THE MYSTERY OF
THE GHOSTLY GALLEON

Trixie
Belden

Your TRIXIE BELDEN Library

Trixie
Belden and the
MYSTERY OF THE
GHOSTLY GALLEON

BY KATHRYN KENNY

Cover by Jack Wacker

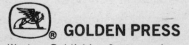 GOLDEN PRESS

Western Publishing Company, Inc.

Racine, Wisconsin

All names, characters, and events in this
story are entirely fictitious.

CONTENTS

THE MYSTERY OF
THE GHOSTLY GALLEON

The Vanishing Pirate · 1

TRIXIE BELDEN GASPED as she collapsed into a chair. "Jeepers, Honey!" she exclaimed breathlessly. "Your news had better be important. You sounded so mysterious on the phone that I dropped everything and ran all the way. I didn't even stop to dry the dinner dishes." She ran an impatient hand through her unruly blond curls.

Her best friend, Honey Wheeler, couldn't help smiling. "I meant for you to hurry over," she said, "but I didn't mean for you to break the Olympic track record, Trix."

Trixie's merry blue eyes twinkled. "I did get here in double-quick time at that, didn't I? You should have seen me, Honey. My feet were flying so fast that dust now covers the entire town of Sleepyside-on-the-Hudson."

In spite of her secret worry, Honey laughed as she sat on the edge of her neat bed.

She was taller and slimmer than Trixie, though both girls were fourteen years old. Honey had long golden hair and wide hazel eyes.

She once had been very lonely, but then one day, her wealthy father had bought the luxurious Manor House in the Hudson Valley, with its stables and lake and acres of rolling green lawns. Almost at once, Honey had met Trixie, who lived with her parents and her three brothers at Crabapple Farm, an attractive white frame house nestled in the hollow below.

Today, thanks to Trixie, Honey had many friends. Besides Trixie's two older brothers, seventeen-year-old Brian and fifteen-year-old Mart, there were wealthy Di Lynch, who was in the same grade as Trixie and Honey, and Dan Mangan. Dan was the nephew of Bill Regan, who looked after the stables and helped run the Wheeler's huge estate.

Honey's parents had also adopted seventeen-year-old Jim Frayne, whom Trixie and Honey had befriended when he ran away from his cruel stepfather.

The seven friends had formed a club known as the Bob-Whites of the Glen, or B.W.G.'s, for short. They tried always to help each other, as well as other people.

Trixie and Honey had solved many exciting mysteries and hoped someday to go into business together as detectives. They were planning to form the Belden-Wheeler Detective Agency.

Now Trixie announced, "If you don't tell me why you asked me to get here in such a hurry, Honey, I'll simply die of curiosity!"

"The thing is," Honey began, "I've got some bad news. Our trip to the Finger Lakes this weekend is off."

Trixie stared. "Off? You mean—we're not going there with your parents after all?"

Miserably, Honey nodded. "I'm afraid that's exactly what I do mean," she said. "My dad's been called out of town on business, and Mom's gone with him. Besides me and Jim, you're the first to know. Oh, Trixie, I'm so sorry! I know you're disappointed. The others will be, too. The Bob-Whites have talked of nothing else all week at school."

Trixie swallowed hard as she gazed around her friend's dainty bedroom with its white ruffled organdy curtains.

"Don't worry about it, Honey," Trixie said at

15

last. "The Bob-Whites will understand. Anyway, there'll be other weekends. . . ." Her voice trailed off into silence as she thought of the plans they'd made.

Every afternoon after school that week, Trixie and the other club members had met in their neat little clubhouse, with its wisteria winding around the door. There they had pored over maps and had looked forward to a weekend of long walks, lazy talks, and tall stories told around a crackling fire.

It was October, a perfect time for flying to the Finger Lakes in northern New York State. The Wheelers owned a cottage on beautiful Owasco Lake, not far from the city of Auburn—but now the Bob-Whites wouldn't get to see it.

Honey rose to her feet and walked to the window. She stared out through the dusk at the tall trees, and at the leaves that were turning bright red and gold.

"There is something else we could do this weekend," she said slowly over her shoulder. "Daddy suggested that we could go to the Catskills instead. We'd have to go tomorrow instead of Saturday, though, and leave right after school."

"Why, Honey Wheeler!" Trixie exclaimed, bounding out of her chair. "But that's perfect!

16

Tomorrow's Friday, and that would work out just fine."

"I know," Honey said. "That's what I thought at first. But now I'm not sure we should go."

Trixie looked perplexed. "Not go? Oh, Honey, why not?"

"Because the person who's going there didn't invite us herself," Honey said in a rush. "I've been worrying about it ever since Daddy left. You see, he knew we'd be disappointed about the canceled trip. So Jim and I think he suggested the first thing that came into his head. He's insisted on paying everyone's expenses, of course."

Trixie stared at her friend. "I still don't understand, Honey. We *can't* go to the Finger Lakes, but we *can* go to the Catskills, except you're not sure we'll be welcome. Is that it?"

Honey turned toward her with a sigh of relief. "That's it, exactly," she said. "I *knew* you'd understand! Jim's not sure we should go, either. So he suggested that I invite you here and—"

She broke off as a light tap sounded on the door. Jim poked his red head into the room. "Have you told her about it?" he asked his sister. "What does Trixie think? Should we foist ourselves on Miss Trask this weekend or not?"

Suddenly Trixie *did* understand what Honey had been trying to tell her. Kind, middle-aged

Miss Trask was one of their favorite people. She had once been Honey's governess, but now that Honey no longer needed her in that capacity, Miss Trask managed the huge Wheeler estate for Honey's father. She also took charge of everything while he was away on his frequent business trips.

This time, when Miss Trask had learned about the canceled plans, Trixie guessed that she had offered to take the Bob-Whites somewhere else instead. Or had she?

When Trixie asked, it was Jim who said, "No, she didn't offer, Trix. It was all Dad's idea. He did ask her about it, of course, and she told him it was fine. But what else could she say?"

"What's more," Honey said, "we think that she was planning something pretty special for herself this weekend. She thought we'd all be away, you see. So she'd planned a trip of her own."

"Where in the Catskills is she going?" Trixie asked.

"That's just it," Honey answered. "She's going home."

Trixie's mouth dropped open in a silent O of surprise. Before this evening, she hadn't really given any thought to the fact that their Miss Trask had any home but the Manor House. But of course she must have come from somewhere.

Trixie knew that she had taught in a girls' school before she worked for the Wheelers. In fact, that was where she had met Honey. Trixie also knew that Miss Trask had an invalid sister whom she helped to support, and who was at that time convalescing in a New York hospital. Miss Trask liked the Bob-Whites and willingly helped when they needed her. She had patiently arranged a wedding while the Bob-Whites were in the middle of searching for a missing heiress and solving mysteries around Glen Road. She had even supervised a charity bazaar while Trixie and Honey were chasing a headless horseman.

Trixie felt guilty as she looked at her friends. "I didn't even know Miss Trask had a home," she said softly.

"We didn't know, either," Honey answered, "until she told Dad about it this afternoon. Oh, Trix, it sounds so nice. She was raised in a place called Pirate's Point, and her childhood home is an old inn."

"It's called Pirate's Inn," Jim added. "It got its name from the original owner, who—are you ready for this?—really was a pirate. He was one of Miss Trask's long-ago relatives, who used the inn as a storage place for his ill-gotten gains."

Honey gasped. "I didn't know that!"

"But it's true," Jim told her, chuckling. "I've just come back from the stables, and Regan told me all about it."

Trixie sighed. "It sounds wonderful."

"Better than a cottage on Owasco Lake?" Jim asked her, grinning.

"Better even than that," Trixie agreed slowly. "But of course you two are right. We can't go. It wouldn't be fair to Miss Trask."

There was silence as the three friends stared glumly at each other.

"Then someone's going to have to tell her," Jim pointed out at last. "We've got to convince her that we've got something better to do right here at home."

"Or else, knowing her, she won't leave us," Honey added quickly. "She's worked so hard for us. Now it's our turn to give her a weekend to herself."

"You two could come and stay with us at Crabapple Farm," Trixie suggested. "Moms and Dad won't mind at all. We can spend the weekend cleaning up the clubhouse and exercising the horses."

There was silence once more as the three tried hard to ignore their intense disappointment.

"I think your idea is a fine one, Trix," Jim said, trying to sound cheerful. "So now there's nothing left to do except find Miss Trask and tell her how we feel."

"She'll probably try to be polite and urge us to go with her," Honey warned, leading the way down the stairs.

"You're right," Jim answered, following close on her heels. "So we mustn't listen. Right, Trix?"

"Right, Jim," Trixie answered. "Nothing she tells us must change our minds."

But when they found Miss Trask, they were surprised when she didn't try to change their minds at all. As usual, she was neatly dressed in a smart tweed suit, and she stood in the living room and quietly listened to everything they had to say. Once Trixie thought she saw a twinkle in her bright blue eyes, but it disappeared so quickly that Trixie thought she must have been mistaken.

"And so, dear Miss Trask," Honey finished at last, "we want you to take your trip the way you'd planned. The Bob-Whites really do have a lot to do right here at home. Isn't that right?" She appealed to the others, who nodded solemnly.

"Very well," Miss Trask declared briskly. "I wouldn't want to talk you into doing anything you didn't want to. So, naturally, it's quite all right if you wish to spend the weekend at Crabapple Farm."

Trixie, Honey, and Jim slowly turned to leave.

"I must admit," Miss Trask remarked to their backs, "I was hoping you'd all help me solve a mystery this weekend. But then, I guess you wouldn't be interested."

"A mystery?" echoed Trixie, swinging around. "What kind of mystery?"

Miss Trask smiled and tucked a stray strand of crisp gray hair behind her ear. "Oh, it happened so long ago that it would probably be a waste of time trying to solve it."

Trixie glanced anxiously at Jim and Honey. "It couldn't do any harm if we just listened to the story for a few minutes, could it?"

Miss Trask didn't give them a chance to answer. "The mystery," she began, "involved a rascally ancestor of mine who was a pirate. I understand that Regan has already told you a little bit about him."

Jim nodded.

"But did you know," Miss Trask continued, "that Captain Trask once disappeared completely in front of a roomful of people?"

Trixie and Honey were by her side instantly.

"What happened?" Trixie asked breathlessly. "Did the pirate really disappear?"

"He really did," Miss Trask replied, smiling. "You see, Captain Trask knew that the soldiers were coming to arrest him. But he refused to let that worry him at all. He sat in the inn's dining room, casually eating lunch. He was even in his shirt sleeves at the time. The soldiers rushed in and surrounded the captain's table and—"

"And did they arrest him?" Jim interrupted, interested in spite of himself.

"No, they never did," Miss Trask answered. "In the next moment, the soldiers had backed away in astonishment. The old captain had completely disappeared! He just wasn't there anymore. To this day, no one has ever discovered how he did it."

"Jeepers!" Trixie breathed. "What a mystery!"

"And did the family ever hear from Captain Trask again?" Honey asked.

"Oh, yes," Miss Trask answered. "That same day, the captain's ship was sighted sailing down the Hudson River. And soon after that, the captain himself arrived in Jamaica. The old rascal had made good his escape, and he lived for many years after that."

"I'll bet there's a secret passage somewhere in that dining room," Trixie said thoughtfully.

"Or a trapdoor under the captain's table," Jim remarked. "It probably leads to the cellar."

"Ah, yes," Miss Trask said, sighing. "There could indeed be either or both of those things somewhere around. When I was a girl, I looked for them, of course. But I never did figure out the answer. Naturally, I hadn't had as much experience as any of you—"

"And were you really hoping we could solve the mystery for you?" Honey asked eagerly.

Miss Trask smiled. "I really was. In fact, I was so sure you'd want to see that old dining room for yourselves that I've already telephoned to say you're all coming."

Trixie took a deep breath. "It sounds so marvelous," she said, fighting temptation, "but we really couldn't—"

Miss Trask looked down at her hands. "I can guess why you have refused to come with me to visit my brother," she said, her voice low. "But your concern is quite unnecessary. I really do hope you'll come with me."

The three friends exchanged startled glances. For one thing, they hadn't realized until now that Miss Trask even had a brother. For another, there was a note of appeal in her voice that they'd never heard before.

To Trixie, she sounded worried at the thought of going alone to her childhood home.

I'm imagining things, Trixie thought. *I must be.*

But she had a sudden hunch that she wasn't.

A Family Quarrel • 2

It was exactly one hour later when Trixie raced home to talk to her parents. Soon afterward, her cheeks still rosy from the crisp night air, she hurried away to find her two older brothers.

She discovered them in the warm and fragrant kitchen of the old farmhouse. Maps lay scattered across the polished surface of the familiar maple table. Trixie guessed they had been busy discussing plans for the coming weekend.

Six-year-old Bobby, Trixie's youngest brother, had long been in bed. Even Reddy, the Beldens' lovable Irish setter, was fast asleep. He lay on the braided rug at Brian's feet and snored softly.

As always, the kitchen looked cozy in the lamplight. Its walls were hung with gleaming copper utensils, and treasured china was proudly displayed on plate racks and cup hooks.

Thinking of china, Trixie glanced guiltily toward the sink. It was now clean and free from the clutter of wet dishes that she had left there earlier. Someone had dried them and put them away. Judging from the exasperated look on Mart's face, Trixie guessed that he was the some-one who'd had to do it.

Brian grunted. "So you're home."

"I'm home," Trixie agreed, hastily deciding not to mention the tender subject of chores. "Brian, Mart, guess what?"

Mart, who was only eleven months older than Trixie, and who looked enough like her to be her twin, immediately closed his eyes. He clapped one hand to his forehead. "Wait!" he droned. "Don't tell us! The One and Only Mart Belden, the All-Knowing, will read it in your cerebral cortex!"

He paused, thoroughly enjoying his use of big words, which he could pronounce but never spell.

"I prognosticate," he droned on, "that we are not going to sojourn at Owasco Lake, after all. It appears that we have had our collective arm

26

twisted. We will instead peregrinate to the Cats-kills to visit Miss Trask's brother, who is, it seems, an innkeeper."

Trixie giggled. "You're right, and wasn't that something? None of us knew Miss Trask even had a brother—"

"Quiet, squaw!" Mart thundered. "I am not finished. Now, where was I? Oh, yes! Can it be that my pea-brained sister seriously expects to ascertain the solution to an ancient mystery? And can the aforesaid mystery have anything to do with an evanescent pirate? If so, I can tell her right now how the mystifying deed was done."

Trixie was startled. "You can?"

"Sure," Mart said in his normal voice. He opened his eyes and grinned at her. "The answer's very simple. The old captain covered himself all over with vanishing cream and became invisible."

"Oh, Mart!" Trixie exclaimed, trying not to laugh. "I suppose Honey called you."

"Nope, it was Jim," Mart said. He opened the big old refrigerator and gazed affectionately at its contents.

Brian ran a hand through his dark, wavy hair. "Jim told us everything," he said. "But whatever happened to not listening to any arguments? What happened to standing firm, no matter

27

what? I thought you guys finally decided to give Miss Trask some time to herself."

"Yes, but—" Trixie began.

"I know what it was," Mart said over his shoulder. "Trixie's been reading one of her dumb spy novels again. What's the woman's name who writes those silly things? Lucy Snodgrass?"

Trixie's face flamed red with indignation. "Her name is Lucy *Radcliffe*. And she does *not* write dumb novels. She's only eighteen years old, but she's had so many wonderful adventures. She's been all over the world in the service of her country, and—"

Mart threw back his head and roared with laughter. "Only eighteen years old, eh? Take it from me, O squaw, that author's had so much happen to her that I'd guess she's seventy years old if she's a day. What's more, I'll bet she has a bit of a mustache."

Trixie swallowed hard. "She doesn't have anything of the kind," she declared loyally. "Lucy is a tall, willowy redhead with a peaches-and-cream complexion. She always describes herself in her books. That's how I know."

"All *I* know," Mart said, "is that you've been just itching for some new adventure recently, Trix. Just like Lucy Snodgrass—"

"Radcliffe," Trixie said, between her teeth.

"And *that's* the real reason you decided the Bob-Whites are going to the Catskills instead of staying home," Mart finished smoothly. He turned toward the table, his hands holding the remains of an apple pie.

All at once, Trixie blinked back hot tears that threatened to spill down her cheeks. In the past few days, she had found Mart's teasing to be almost unbearable. She found herself wondering whether Miss Trask had ever been forced to endure similar torture. It was certainly strange that she had never before mentioned her brother to any of them.

"Oh, Mart," she exclaimed, her voice trembling, "it wasn't like that at all. The real reason we agreed to go with Miss Trask was that I had a sudden feeling that she needed us."

"I'll bet," Mart said sarcastically.

"Knock it off, Mart!" Brian said quickly.

But it was too late. Mart seemed to be too enchanted with the sound of his own voice to stop now. "I can see it all," he announced. "Trixie Teenybopper is simply yearning for adventure, just like her fictional heroine—she of the bee-yootiful complexion—"

Trixie was suddenly furious. "My Lucy books are no dumber than those Cosmo McNaught science-fiction things you're always reading."

"It's not the same thing at all," Mart drawled, cutting himself a huge wedge of pie. "Cosmo is a superlative writer, and moreover, he's not covered with adolescent zits."

Trixie could feel the hot tears gathering behind her eyelids. She swallowed hard. *I won't let Mart make me cry*, she told herself. *I just won't!* All the same, she knew she was going to have to run to the blessed privacy of her own room—and soon.

"I'm going to bed," she said abruptly. "And by the way, you needn't worry about tomorrow's arrangements, either of you. Dad, Moms, and the other Bob-Whites have already been told about the plans for the trip."

"Thank you, 'Lucy' Belden—" Mart began.

Reddy raised his head in sleepy outrage as Brian suddenly rose to his feet and shoved his chair roughly toward the table. "Sometimes, Mart," he said, "you go too far. And Trixie's right! I don't think that Lucy Radcliffe's *Adventure in Paris* is one bit sillier than Cosmo McNaught's *Journey to the Crab Nebula.*"

Mart flushed at the unaccustomed criticism from his older brother. "It's not the same thing at all," he mumbled.

Trixie was already halfway out the door. But she was gratified to hear Brian add, "And one other thing, Mart—if I were you, I wouldn't be quite so quick to poke fun at Trixie's sudden hunches. If you'll think back, you'll realize they're usually right!"

During school the next morning, Trixie tried hard to forget her quarrel with Mart. She kept telling herself that he hadn't meant to hurt her feelings. All the same, she found it difficult to concentrate on her lessons. Several times, when she should have been studying, she found herself, instead, staring miserably out of the window.

By lunchtime, her spirits were so low that she was even wishing she could stay home, after all.

No one seemed to notice her long face, however, when she hurried into the noisy cafeteria. Brian and Jim, dressed in white caps and aprons, were on duty that day. At the moment, though, they were seated at a table with the other Bob-Whites. They were snatching a few moments to make sure everyone understood the final arrangements. Trixie stood still, listening to them.

"All right," Jim was saying, raising his voice over the excited chatter going on around him. "Is everything clear? The station wagon is already loaded and ready to go. Miss Trask will drive it here and meet us outside, right after school. Okay?"

Trixie thought of the Bob-Whites' station wagon, of which they each owned exactly a one-seventh share. She also thought of her small weekend case, which the boys had placed inside it earlier that morning. Besides her clothes, the case contained the latest Lucy Radcliffe spy thriller. Trixie had packed it while Mart wasn't looking. Now she wished she hadn't. She didn't care if she never ever read another Lucy Radcliffe adventure.

Dan Mangan solemnly nodded his dark head. "How long will it take us to get to Pirate's Point?" he asked.

"Miss Trask says it'll take us less than two hours," Honey told him. "Apparently it's not all that far away."

"Well, it all sounds perfectly perfect to me," declared Di Lynch, her violet eyes shining. With the curtain of long, dark hair that framed her pretty face, she was, Trixie always thought, the best-looking girl in the ninth grade.

"Just think," Di continued. "We're going to an old inn, and already there's a mystery for Trixie to solve—"

"And what else could we wish for?" Honey added happily.

Trixie could think of something else to wish for, but she bit back the reply that sprang to her lips. She looked bitterly across at Mart, but he avoided her eye.

"I have to admit," Dan said, "that our trip today sounds almost too good to be true. I still can't believe I've got this whole weekend off. I keep on feeling I should be back home, helping with the chores."

Trixie remembered the time when Dan had not been the happy boy he was today. Once he had lived in the city. There he had gotten in with the wrong crowd; then his uncle, Bill Regan, had brought him to Sleepyside-on-the-Hudson. Now Dan lived and worked with the Wheelers' gamekeeper, Mr. Maypenny.

"All right, then," Brian said briskly. "Everything's all set. Are there any more questions?"

Mart rose slowly to his feet. "I've got a question to ask," he said. "It's kind of important."

"Come on, then! Out with it!" Brian exclaimed impatiently.

Mart hesitated as he looked up at last and caught Trixie's eye. She held her breath when she saw the sheepish look on his face.

Why, she thought with astonishment, *I do believe my almost-twin is sorry about our quarrel last night. He's going to ask me to forgive him for being so mean.*

At that moment, however, Jerry Vanderhoef,

33

at the next table, leaned toward them. "For cry-ing out loud, Belden!" he yelled. "What's the question? My friends and I can't wait to hear it." He waved a casual hand at the group of grinning students who were just taking their places around him.

At first, Mart stiffened. Then the expression on his face changed as he grinned back at them. "Never let it be said that Mart the Magnificent would disappoint an audience," he answered, with a sweeping bow. "This is the question: You're standing in a house. There are windows on all four sides of it. Every window faces south. Suddenly, a bear walks by. What color is the bear?"

Jerry looked incredulous. "That's it? That's the important question?"

"Sure," Mart answered. "What else would it be?" Then he hurried away to join the food line.

Di chuckled. "Oh, that Mart! He's always clowning around. What color was the bear, any-way?"

"Don't look at me," Dan said, backing away in mock horror. "I don't have any idea."

"Me, either," Honey added. "Riddles never were my best subject."

"In that case," Jim said, smiling, "I guess we've just found another puzzle for Trixie to solve. You know, gang, if it weren't for our female sleuth here, we wouldn't have half the fun we do."

Suddenly Trixie felt better as she smiled back at her loyal friends. As her spirits lifted, she made herself a silent promise. In the days to come, she would do her best not to get so upset at Mart's teasing.

Meanwhile, there was much to look forward to. It was Friday. It was a beautiful day. She was about to leave on an exciting trip. And she had a brand-new Lucy Radcliffe adventure to read.

Honey slipped her hand through her friend's arm. "Trix," she said, "do you know what color the bear was?"

Trixie grinned at her. "Nope," she said cheerfully, "I haven't the foggiest notion. But I'll tell you one thing, Honey. I'll figure it out if it's the last thing I do!"

She sighed happily. Di was right. It was going to be a perfectly perfect weekend, after all—she hoped.

Mart's Ghost · 3

AFTER THAT, everything seemed to go better for Trixie. Once lunch was over, the minutes seemed to fly by. When the last bell rang to signal the end of the school day, Trixie could hardly credit her own good luck. Her teachers had given her no weekend homework.

"I simply don't believe it," Trixie told Honey as the two girls hurried through the school's large front doors. "No math, no English composition, no anything!"

Honey chuckled and squeezed her arm. "So the only things you've got to worry about are vanishing pirates and wandering bears."

"I've been thinking about that pirate story," Trixie said thoughtfully. "Do you suppose Miss Trask made it up just to get us to go with her?"

"No, I don't," Honey answered promptly. "She told Jim and me about it again last night, after you'd gone home. Apparently, the legend is well known in the area of Pirate's Point. Miss Trask says it's been a real tourist attraction over the years. People who come to the inn are always determined to solve the puzzle."

"But so far nobody has?"

"Miss Trask doesn't know of anyone," Honey said slowly. "But you know, Trix, it's a funny thing. I have an idea she hasn't visited there in a long time. What's more, she didn't seem to want to talk about it. I don't know why."

Trixie didn't know why, either. As she ran to the station wagon moments later, she glanced sharply at Miss Trask, hoping to be able to detect something from her manner. But Miss Trask appeared to be as brisk and efficient as ever. Her face wore the same kindly expression it always did, and Trixie learned nothing.

"All set, girls?" Miss Trask asked, smiling from her seat behind the wheel. "Of course, I'm sure you've been ready ever since school started this morning. As soon as the others get here, we can be on our way." She chuckled. "The boys

37

have actually agreed to let me drive, since I know the way. Wasn't that nice of them?"

Still smiling and talking, she watched while Trixie and Honey made themselves comfortable beside her. Then she waited patiently until, one by one, the rest of the Bob-Whites arrived.

There was the usual confusion concerning who was going to sit where. Finally, Mart and Dan settled the argument by scrambling to the back of the wagon. There they stuck their legs out in front of them and beamed triumphantly, while Di, Brian, and Jim climbed into the remaining seats.

Through all the excitement, Miss Trask smiled serenely. It was as if she hadn't a care in the world.

There was, Trixie was beginning to discover, more to Miss Trask than met the eye.

There was no mystery concerning Miss Trask's abilities as a driver, however. They were excellent, as the Bob-Whites already knew. Under her expert handling, the station wagon was soon moving smoothly along the highway, and before long, they had left Sleepyside far behind them.

"Yo-ho-ho, and a bottle of pop!" Mart sang out suddenly, breaking a long silence. "Pirate's Inn, here we come! I don't know about you guys, but I find the suspense absolutely excruciating!"

"What suspense?" Di asked.

"Aha, me fair beauty," Mart said, stroking an imaginary mustache, "you may well ask. The suspense concerns—" he paused dramatically— "the ghost of Captain Trask."

Dan frowned. "I didn't know the inn was supposed to have a ghost."

"Oh, I haven't heard that it does," Mart answered cheerfully. "But if it doesn't now, it soon will have. You see, I've given the matter a lot of thought. And I've figured out a way to solve, once and for all, the mystery of the old captain's disappearance."

Brian sighed heavily. "I know I'm going to get a silly answer," he said, "but then, I'm going to ask a silly question. How are you going to solve the mystery, O All-Knowing One?"

"First we must summon the captain's ghost from its watery grave," Mart answered. "Then we'll give him the third degree. You know— we've seen it done in the late-night movies lots of times. We'll simply sit him down, shine a light into his ghostly eyes, and interrogate him relentlessly. 'Where were you when the dastardly deed was done?' we'll demand to know. Take my word for it. It can't fail."

"I'm sorry to disappoint you, Mart," Miss Trask remarked, with a twinkle in her eye, "but

TRIXIE BELDEN

I just don't think that will work. For one thing, I'm afraid the captain didn't go to a watery grave. I seem to remember hearing that he died in bed. For another, he was in Jamaica at the time. I must say, though, it's nice to hear your voice at last. You've been so quiet for so long that I wondered if you were still with us."

"Oh, he's still with us," Trixie couldn't resist saying. "He's just been suffering from a condition known as severe guilty conscience."

She knew it was a mistake as soon as the words were out of her mouth. She tried to think of some way to take them back, but it was too late.

Di giggled. "Why, Mart! *Do* you have a guilty conscience?"

"Yes, Mart," Dan added, "tell us about it. What did you do?"

"Hold it," Mart said. "I do *not* have a guilty conscience. My *little* sister is just mad because she doesn't know the answer to my bear riddle. I don't know why she's so upset—even her beloved Lucy Snodgrass couldn't solve that mystery. But Trixie always gets a bit peevish when she's frustrated."

In an instant, Trixie forgot all the promises she had made to herself. Furious, she turned and glared at her brother and tried desperately to think of a crushing reply.

Before she could, however, Brian asked hastily, *"Is* there a ghost at the inn, Miss Trask?"

There was a long pause. Then, to Trixie's astonishment, Miss Trask answered slowly, "To be honest, Brian, I don't really know. You see, my brother, Frank, has made so many changes. . . ."

Trixie promptly forgot everything she had been about to say to her almost-twin. She was too busy puzzling over this last remark.

What a peculiar thing for Miss Trask to say! Trixie thought. *Why couldn't she answer Brian's question?* Surely it had been simple enough. Was there or wasn't there a ghost at the inn? And what did Miss Trask's brother have to do with it, anyway?

Trixie sighed. "There are times," she said softly to Honey, "when I don't think there are nearly enough answers in the whole wide world to satisfy my curiosity."

"Be patient, Trix," Honey told her.

"I've never been any good at being patient," Trixie confessed. "I hate having to sit and wait for things to happen."

"I know," Honey answered, remembering how hard Trixie had worked to solve the many mysteries they had been involved in.

"Oh, Honey!" Trixie exclaimed. "There are times when I wish I hadn't been born with such an inquis—inquis—nosy mind. Why do you suppose I was?"

But to that question, Honey was sure there was no answer at all.

As the Bob-Whites neared their destination, they saw the beautiful Catskill Mountains loom before them. Trixie caught her breath as the station wagon turned into a graveled driveway. They had arrived at last at Pirate's Inn.

Set back from a cliff overlooking the wide Hudson River, the old two-story building was everything she'd hoped it would be.

Its dark timbers looked warm and inviting. Tall trees reached toward its three-gabled roof. Leaded panes sparkled in the golden rays of the afternoon sun. And behind a large bay window on the ground floor, Trixie could see the vague outlines of people seated around tables. The area was—it had to be—the mysterious dining room.

"Why, the inn is beautiful!" she exclaimed, opening the car door and jumping out.

"Simply perfect!" Di agreed behind her.

"Oh, Miss Trask," Honey asked softly, "how could you ever bear to leave a place like this?"

Miss Trask came and stood beside them. "It's not always possible to live where one wants to," she answered quietly. "And sometimes there are other things—and other people—who are more important. Sometimes, you see, there's not enough money in a family to take care of—of certain responsibilities. And when that happens, why, someone in that family has to go out and earn a living."

Trixie guessed that Miss Trask was talking about her invalid sister, who needed such constant care and attention.

"Do you ever wish you didn't have to work for my family at the Manor House?" Honey asked in a small voice. She sounded as if she dreaded hearing the answer.

At once, Miss Trask turned swiftly and gave her a quick hug. "Oh, my, no, Honey!" she said briskly. "I have never been one who wastes time thinking about what might have been. Besides, what on earth would I do without you and Jim to keep me on my toes?"

Satisfied with the answer, Honey smiled and turned to help unload the luggage. At the same moment, Trixie gasped.

The inn's front doors had suddenly swung open, and a figure stood motionless on the top step.

That he was a pirate, there was no doubt at all. A three-cornered hat sat squarely on his head. His rosy-cheeked face wore a black, bushy beard.

From his brass-buttoned coat to his brown knee-length boots, he seemed to Trixie to have stepped straight out of the pages of a history book.

She wasn't the only one to think so. Behind her, she heard Mart draw a deep breath. "Gleeps!" he sputtered finally. "He managed to get here from Jamaica, after all. He's come to welcome us to Pirate's Inn! It's the ghost of Captain Trask!"

Ready for Action · 4

FOR WHAT SEEMED to be an endless moment, the apparition and the Bob-Whites stood staring at each other. Then the figure moved, and the spell was broken. He hurried toward them with both hands outstretched.

"Well, well, me hearties!" he boomed. "So you managed to get here, eh? I didn't recognize the wagon, you see, so I wasn't sure if it was really you." He turned to Miss Trask and gripped her hands. "Marge, it's good to see you. It's been a long time."

The "ghost" was obviously none other than Miss Trask's brother, Frank.

Now that he was close to them, and in spite of the beard, Trixie could see the family resemblance. He was only slightly taller than his sister. But as he doffed his three-cornered hat to all of them, Trixie could see that his head was the same shape as Miss Trask's and that he had the same crisp iron-gray hair. His twinkling blue eyes even had the same laugh lines at their corners.

Miss Trask had been frowning at her brother in disapproval. "I almost didn't recognize you in those outlandish clothes, Frank," she said sharply. "And Mart, here, thought you were a ghost. Honey, Trixie, Di, Jim, Brian, Mart, Dan—this is my brother."

Mr. Trask didn't seem to mind at all that his sister didn't like his pirate costume. He chuckled. "So you thought I was a ghost, eh, Mart? Ah, me bucko, and that's just what you were supposed to think. It gives the old place a bit of atmosphere, you see. And that's what the tourists pay for."

Trixie chuckled. "I bet Mart was hoping you really *were* Captain Trask," she said as Mart turned red with embarrassment.

"And if I had been, I'll bet he'd have been planning to ask me how I disappeared," Frank Trask said, grinning. "Now, that's what I like! A boy with brains! But come on, now! Shake a leg! Your rooms are ready and waiting. No doubt

46

you'll be wanting a wash and a brushup before the galley serves up your afternoon snacks. You're to order what you want. It's on the house."

Mart's face brightened at once. "Snacks?"

"In the dining room?" Trixie asked eagerly.

Mr. Trask turned to the station wagon and began to unload it rapidly. "Snacks in the dining room now," he promised, "and dinner later. At eight o'clock, you're all invited to dine at the captain's table with Marge and me. Tonight we're celebrating something special."

At once, Jim looked worried. "If it's a family celebration, sir, I really don't think we ought to intrude."

"Fiddlesticks!" Mr. Trask boomed, striding rapidly toward the inn and carrying most of the luggage. "Now, would I have invited you if I didn't want you? The fact is, I've got a fine surprise to share. Yessirree! A fine surprise!"

Miss Trask stood for a moment staring after him. Then she sighed and said, "For once I agree with my brother. You wouldn't have been invited here if you weren't wanted. And I don't want to have to repeat that every ten minutes this weekend." She smiled for the first time since they had arrived. "Is that clear, me hearties?"

Jim chuckled. "Aye-aye, ma'am."

"But, all the same," Honey remarked, "we didn't realize you were celebrating something special tonight."

Miss Trask frowned. "Neither did I!" she said.

Minutes later, Trixie and Honey stood enchanted in the doorway of their bedroom on the second floor. It was as if they were about to step into a ship's cabin. From the paneled walls, lined with prints of long-ago sailing ships, to the neat bunk beds and blue sailcloth curtains at the windows, the effect was a delightful one.

When Trixie crossed the room and peeked outside, she saw that it overlooked the inn's front entrance. As she watched, red and yellow leaves from a tall maple tree drifted gently to the ground. Beyond, the setting sun turned the Hudson River to gold.

"Oh, how lovely," Trixie said softly.

"Isn't it perfect?" Honey asked, gently testing the bottom bunk.

Trixie sighed happily. "It really is."

A small bathroom connected their room with Di's. Soon the three girls were excitedly visiting back and forth.

"Have you seen the boys' rooms?" Di asked. "I don't know how they did it, but Brian and Mart seem to have been given the captain's cabin. It has brass lamps and everything! Jim and Dan have a room like ours."

"I wonder where Miss Trask's room is," Trixie said. "I know she came upstairs with us, but then I sort of lost track of her."

"Her room's at the end of this passage," Honey answered. "I caught sight of it before I came in here. I don't know if she wanted it that way, but it isn't a bit like this."

"What is it like?" Di asked.

Honey shrugged. "It's just a regular old room. There's no nautical theme in it or anything—just some big, dark furniture and a small single bed."

"Maybe it's the room she's always had ever since she was a child," Trixie said thoughtfully. "And did you notice what she said downstairs? '*For once* I agree with my brother,' she told us. It almost sounds as if the two of them don't always get along with each other."

Di smiled. "You should be able to understand that, Trix. You don't always get along with yours."

Trixie's face went red. Of course, Di was right. All the same, Trixie wished she hadn't mentioned it. There were times when she knew she fought too much with Mart. There were also times when she would have liked to keep family quarrels private. She knew it was often her own fault that they weren't.

49

Honey had been watching Trixie's face. "If we took fast showers," she said quickly, trying to change the subject, "we could get out of our school clothes and climb into something more comfortable. Then we could go downstairs and get something to eat."

"You've just said the magic words," Trixie announced, throwing her a grateful glance. "I'm starved!"

Di walked back into her own room, but she left the connecting doors open. "The dining room is really neat, too," she called. "Wait till you see it. I only took a quick peek, but it's all done in dark wood. It has brass lamps on the tables, anchors on the walls, and thick red carpeting on the floor."

"Even under the captain's table?" Trixie asked, disappointed. She still had high hopes of finding a trapdoor under there.

"No," said Di, laughing. "It's the only spot in the whole room that doesn't have it. And wait till you see the oil painting!"

"What oil painting?" Honey asked.

But Di wouldn't tell her. "It'll give you the creeps" was all she'd say.

When Trixie, dressed in clean jeans and blouse, reached the dining room at last, she saw immediately what Di meant. On the far wall, lit by a spotlight, was an enormous oil painting of a tall, fierce pirate chief standing guard over his treasure chest. He glared at Trixie, no matter where she moved to in the room.

"What do you think of that, eh?" a voice boomed in her ear.

Startled, Trixie turned and saw Mr. Trask, still in his pirate costume, standing beside her.

"Oh—uh—it's very nice," Trixie stammered.

"Nice! What's nice about it?" Mr. Trask asked, laughing. "It's supposed to scare the living be-jabbers out of you, me hearty. It's also supposed to be Captain Trask. As you can see, he's guard-ing the family treasure." He smiled to himself. "In fact, Trixie, he's guarding more than some people think."

"Did he really look like that?" Trixie asked.

"Well, now, since you ask me," Mr. Trask answered softly, "no, he didn't. But don't tell anyone. The old painting we had of the real cap-tain was the same size as that one. But in real life, the old captain didn't look nearly fierce enough. In fact, he looked like a real softy. So I had a new portrait painted to me own specifi-cations, you see." He sighed and shook his head sadly. "I know that Marge won't like it, though. No, she won't like it at all. She doesn't go much for the changes I've made around here. But in my opinion, the new painting gives the place—"

"Atmosphere?" Trixie suggested, smiling.

"Exactly!" Mr. Trask exclaimed. "But there! Enough of this jibber-jabber, girl. Go and join your friends. The captain's table is occupied right now, but you'll sit at it tonight, I promise. This afternoon, though, I've assigned one of my best waiters to take your order, so go ahead and enjoy yourselves."

He hurried away, and Trixie moved slowly to a long table in the big bay window. There the rest of the Bob-Whites were waiting for her. They smiled as they saw that her eyes were fixed on what was obviously the captain's table. It was large and round and obviously very old. It stood in the exact center of the room. The glow from the room's subdued lighting reflected softly in its polished surface.

Seated at it were three adults and four teen-aged boys. The boys appeared to be spending more time under the table than they did in their chairs. Trixie could see them busily tapping different areas of the bare, polished wood floor. She could tell they were looking for a trapdoor of some kind. She found herself hoping passionately that they wouldn't find anything.

"All right, folks, what'll it be?" a gloomy voice asked over her head.

Trixie looked up quickly and gasped. Standing by her side was one of the most villainous-looking men she had ever seen in her life. Dressed as a pirate, he was more frightening by far than the painting of Captain Trask.

He was tall and skinny. He wore a black patch over one eye and a red scarf around his head. A gray stubble of beard covered his chin.

Someone should tell him to smarten up, Trixie thought.

As if he could read her mind, he said wearily, "Dumb outfit, ain't it?" He pointed with the end of his pencil to his red and white striped T-shirt. "But I gotta wear it. Rule of the house. I'm also supposed to tell you that I'm Weasel Willis, and I'm your waiter for this afternoon. Of course, the name's not really Weasel, but that's another dumb rule. We all gotta have nicknames. So what'll it be?"

Honey frowned. "What do you suggest?"

"Since you ask me," Weasel said, "I don't suggest anything. You probably won't like the food here, anyway. This afternoon, everyone seems to want the Cannonball Pie. At least, that's what they've been ordering. But it's probably no good."

"If everyone's been ordering it," Di said firmly, "then I'm sure it's excellent. Er—what is it?"

"It's just a fancy name for a cherry tart," Weasel answered. "It's supposed to be a specialty of the house. At least, that's what Cookie likes to believe."

Mart stared, fascinated. "Cookie?"

"The chef," Weasel said briefly, then stood with his pencil poised in resignation over his order pad. He seemed to know that he was about to receive seven orders for Cannonball Pie.

He was right.

When he had gone to fetch the food, Trixie leaned across the table and said, "If that's supposed to be one of Mr. Trask's best waiters, I wonder what his worst ones are like?"

"Maybe we ought to tell Mr. Trask what that waiter is really like," Dan said.

"On the other hand," Honey replied, "perhaps we should have taken Weasel's advice and ordered something else."

But a short while later, when seven plates had been hastily scraped clean, the verdict was unanimous. The tart, in spite of its peculiar name, was the most delicious they had ever tasted. The pastry melted in the mouth, the whipped cream topping was perfection, and the cherry filling itself surpassed any superlative that Mart could think of.

He summoned their waiter at once. "You

shouldn't tell people they won't enjoy it," he announced severely, pushing his almost clean empty plate away. "That delectable morsel really hit the spot, you know."

But all Weasel said was, "Oh, well, maybe the chef had a good day for once. He doesn't often. Sometimes he gets homesick, and when that happens, his cooking's terrible."

"Where's he from?" Trixie asked.

"Someplace called the Cordon Bleu," Weasel answered.

"But that's a very famous cooking school in France!" Di exclaimed. "No wonder the food is so excellent."

"You couldn't prove it by me," Weasel said sourly.

Brian watched as he joined the other pirate waiters on the far side of the room. "Reverse psychology," he said suddenly. "He was using reverse psychology on all of us." He grinned. "Effective, wasn't it?"

"I don't understand what you mean, Brian," Di said.

Brian rubbed his nose thoughtfully. "Don't you see? Sometimes when you tell someone to do something, they immediately do the opposite."

"And I suppose it also works the other way around," Dan said.

"Sure," Brian answered. "For instance, Weasel definitely told us *not* to order the pie. But he also managed to sneak in the information that it was a specialty of the house and that everyone liked it and was ordering it. So what did we order?"

"Scrumptious Cannonball Whatnot!" Mart exclaimed. "Hey, you're right! Weasel's reverse psychology worked like a charm. I only wish I could duplicate his efforts."

"It's too bad you're not that clever," Trixie remarked without thinking.

To her surprise, Mart only sighed. "I know," he said. "But in the meantime, what do you all say to a tour of the town? The fresh air will do us all good. Miss Trask says it's only a few minutes away, and a walk will help Miss Sherlock Belden sharpen her wits. I know she wants to think about the color of a certain bear."

"That's where you're wrong, smarty!" Trixie answered, immediately on the defensive. "I want to stay right here and solve the mystery of the pirate's disappearance!"

Mart chuckled and rose to his feet. "See?" he said to the other grinning Bob-Whites. "I've just shown you how to get rid of a sister in one easy lesson. Reverse psychology really works. It's easy when you know how!"

"Trixie?" Honey asked in a low voice. "Would you like me to stay and help you?"

"Yes, I would," Trixie replied loudly. "And that isn't reverse psychology at all. It's just the truth, which some people I know would never be able to recognize, anyway."

She glared at her brother's back as he sauntered away.

"Don't be angry, Trixie," Honey begged. "You know Mart's only teasing."

But Trixie wasn't listening to Honey. She was busy watching the people at the captain's table.

They were preparing to leave at last. The disappointed looks on their faces told anyone who cared to know that they hadn't found anything.

Honey had noticed them, too. "Don't worry, Trix," she whispered. "They just couldn't have been looking in the right place."

"I know," Trixie answered slowly. "But somehow I feel certain that we'll do better. Come on, Honey. It's time we went into action!"

A Narrow Escape · 5

AFTERWARD, TRIXIE was never quite sure what happened. She thought that she and Honey had moved immediately to claim the mysterious captain's table. Before they reached it, however, they found that a young man with sandy-colored hair was already seated there.

"Oh, woe, Honey! We're too late!" Trixie whispered in dismay. "I don't know how that man managed to move so fast."

She jumped when Mr. Trask's voice said in her ear, "So he beat you to it, did he? Somehow I thought he would. That's Mr. Marvin Appleton, one of our guests. He's had his eye on that table all afternoon. I've been watching him. He's been pretending he's not at all interested in this vanishing pirate business. But mark my words! Before too long, he'll be tapping around under there with the best of 'em. O' course now, if you were to ask me, I'd say he's not going to find the solution that easily. Plenty of people have tried— meself included. But nobody's figured it out yet." He shook his head. "No, girls, the answer's not that simple."

Even while he was speaking, Trixie had been thinking the same thing. It was strange that, in all these years, no one had been able to solve the old mystery.

She closed her eyes and imagined she was back in that long-ago time. The dining room would have looked newer then. It was almost certain there had been no wall-to-wall carpet on the floor. Had the bare wood echoed to the sound of tramping feet as the soldiers marched in to arrest Captain Trask? If so, that old pirate, seated at his table, would have looked up in anticipation as they came toward him.

But what would he have done next? Trixie opened her eyes and stared at the old floorboards under that selfsame table. She noticed that Mr. Appleton seemed to be furtively testing them with the toes of his shoes.

59

When he saw her watching him, he blushed furiously, leaned back in his chair, and pretended to be deeply interested in an old ship's lamp that hung from the ceiling.

Trixie's thoughts began to race. Everyone believed there was a trapdoor under the table. In fact, when Jim first heard the story, it was the first thing that had leaped to his mind.

But what if everyone was wrong?

If there was a trapdoor, why hadn't the soldiers seen Captain Trask hastily flip it open and disappear beneath it? And why hadn't they just as promptly followed him to wherever it led?

Trixie allowed her thoughts to return to her own first guess. She remembered another time and another place, when she had been trying to solve the mystery of some emeralds. There, at the house known as Green Trees, she had searched a wall's dark paneling—and she had found a secret passage. It was entirely possible that there was one here at Pirate's Inn, too, just waiting to be discovered.

"Would you mind if Honey and I explored the rest of the dining room?" she asked Mr. Trask.

"Explore wherever you like, Trixie," he answered, smiling. "We're not busy now, and I've got some things to see to for tonight's little celebration. I just ask that you stay out of the kitchen.

We'll undoubtedly have our usual dinner rush this evening, and Cookie gets a mite upset when he's interrupted."

When he had gone, Honey asked, "Did you think of something, Trix? Have you figured out how Captain Trask disappeared?"

"Do you remember how I thought there might be a secret passage somewhere in these walls?" Trixie asked. "Well, I still think so. And I know just where we're going to start looking."

With Honey close on her heels, Trixie walked quickly to the other side of the large old room. She found herself close to the kitchen, where she could hear a low murmur of voices and the occasional clatter of pots and pans.

She also found something else. A large wooden screen shielded the darkest corner from view. Trixie had noticed it as soon as she had entered the dining room. Now, with a sense of rising excitement, she stepped behind it. She saw at once that the paneling there appeared to be a slightly different color from its neighbors.

"Look at this, Honey!" Trixie exclaimed excitedly, running her fingers lightly over the wood. "I just knew we'd find something. Be patient, now. It'll probably take a while. . . ."

But it took no time at all. Waist-high from the floor, her searching fingers found a depression

61

in the wood's smooth surface. She lifted, and the panel slid noiselessly upward.

Trixie stared at what appeared to be a small wooden cupboard.

"I've found it!" she cried. "Oh, Honey, don't you see? This is how the pirate escaped. He must have climbed in here—and then—" She stopped, frowning. "But I wonder where he went next?"

Honey peered over Trixie's shoulder. "Why," she said, "this is a dumbwaiter. It's one of those things that work on a pulley, I'm sure. Old houses often had them. The servants used to put hot food inside it. Then they hauled on the rope to lift the whole thing upstairs."

"Or to send it downstairs to the cellar?" Trixie asked thoughtfully.

Honey nodded. "Where there's probably another secret way out that leads to a beach."

The two girls stared at each other.

"In that case," Trixie said at last, "there's only one way to find out."

"You're not thinking of getting inside this thing and going down there, are you?" asked Honey, sounding worried.

"Mr. Trask said we could explore where we wanted," Trixie pointed out. Gingerly, she tested the rope. "Anyway, I'm sure it's quite safe. And just think, Honey, if we find out for sure—"

"Then we've solved the mystery!" Honey's hazel eyes were shining.

"And I'll have shown Mart that I'm not as pea-brained as he thinks I am," Trixie said smugly.

Five minutes later, Trixie was heartily thankful that her brother wasn't around to laugh at her. She was positively, definitely, absolutely stuck at the bottom of the shaft!

Curled around in the dumbwaiter's tiny space, she knew she must look like some enormous chick about to burst out of its shell. She only wished she could!

Up until now, everything had worked perfectly. With Honey's nervous hands guiding the rope, the little wooden cupboard had descended easily and quietly. Then, with a gentle bump, it had reached its destination.

But there was no panel here to slide open to her touch. All she could see in front of her was a brick wall.

And now Honey couldn't pull her back up!

"It's no use, Trix," Honey's miserable voice floated down to her. "The rope simply won't move. I think you're too heavy. Isn't there any way you can get out down there?"

With some difficulty, Trixie freed one hand. She ran her fingers over the brick face.

She groaned and tried to fight the feeling of panic that washed over her. "Oh, Honey!" she cried. "There's nothing here at all. It's been closed off. I—I think you're going to have to get someone to help. Oh, please hurry!"

There was a long silence, while Trixie strained her ears to hear what was going on.

At last she heard Honey's voice cry frantically, "Trix? I can't find anyone—not even in the kitchen. You're not going to believe this, but everyone seems to have disappeared, even that funny little man who was sitting at the captain's table."

"But—but that's impossible!" Trixie exclaimed. "Oh, Honey! What are we going to do?"

There was another long silence as Honey rushed away for another search. Trixie tried hard not to think about what would happen if it was unsuccessful. Where could everyone have gone?

The air inside the shaft seemed fresh enough, although Trixie couldn't be sure. Too, one leg was tucked firmly beneath her, and it was horribly cramped. Trixie tried to move it, but it was wedged in tightly.

Mart was right, Trixie thought miserably. *I'm nothing but a pea-brain, after all!*

Suddenly, from somewhere far above her, a door banged, and a woman's voice said, "I don't know what to believe anymore, Frank. All I know is that you've had wild ideas before, and they haven't worked. I—I almost couldn't bear to come home this time—"

"But this time it's different, Marge," a man insisted. "This idea *has* worked. And from now on, things are going to be a lot better, you mark my words."

Trixie felt almost faint with relief as she realized that the two people were Miss Trask and her brother. She guessed they must be standing on the second floor landing. She also guessed they had to be close to the shaft where she was trapped. She opened her mouth to call to them.

Before she could call, however, Miss Trask said sharply, "I've marked your words before, Frank. The last time I was here, we quarreled because you had some wild idea of turning the inn into a fast-food outlet. It was going to have jukeboxes and neon signs and heaven knows what else besides. I don't know what would have happened if the historical society hadn't stepped in and prevented it."

Trixie heard Mr. Trask chuckle. "Ah, you've got me there. That one was a bad idea. But I tell you, Marge, this time I've found the magic formula, and I haven't upset the historical society a bit. I'm giving the people what they want, too. And they're eating it up. All I had to do was to borrow some money and spruce the old place up a bit—"

"You borrowed money?" Miss Trask sounded shocked.

"Which I am about to pay back this very weekend." Her brother's voice was triumphant. "My note's due tomorrow night at seven o'clock. That's why I asked you here. I wanted to prove to you that your brother could do it. And I wanted to see the look on your face when I hand over the cash to our old friend, Nicholas Morgan."

Miss Trask gasped. "You borrowed from *Nick?*"

"And why not?" her brother answered. "He's as rich as Croesus, and he owns a lot of the property around here. He was real friendly when I asked him for a loan."

"I'll just bet he was." Miss Trask's voice sounded bitter. "And if the money isn't paid back? What happens then?"

"Then the place is his," Frank Trask said, "lock, stock, and vanishing pirate. I had to put up the inn as collateral, y'see. But it won't happen, I promise you. I've got the money in a safe place, never fear."

"You haven't got it in *cash!*"

"Of course it's in cash," her brother answered. "You know how I feel about banks, Marge. Don't approve of 'em—never have—never will."

Trixie put her hands over her ears and tried to stop listening. She didn't quite know what to do. Should she clear her throat loudly to let them know that someone was listening, however reluctantly, to their private conversation? Should she yell for help at the top of her lungs?

At that moment, a sudden jerk on the rope beside her solved her problem.

Slowly but surely, Trixie felt herself being pulled up and up. Gradually, the bricked-up hatchway slid downward. She saw floor joists and wooden beams. Then the dining room's dark paneling appeared once more.

Now that she was on the point of being rescued, she could feel the hot tears gathering behind her eyelids, and she realized how frightened she had been.

She twisted her head upward to catch the first sight of her gallant rescuer—and she found herself gazing into the villainous-looking face of Weasel Willis.

Fire! · 6

To Trixie's immense relief, Honey's worried face appeared almost immediately at Weasel's shoulder.

"Are you all right?" she cried, helping her friend to uncurl herself. "Oh, Trix, you have no idea how scared I was. I thought we'd never get you out of there!"

"It's a good thing I wasn't too far away," Weasel remarked mournfully. "Otherwise, I can't think what would have happened." He watched Trixie trying to restore the circulation to her cramped limbs. "Of course, I'm not surprised," he added. "Heaven only knows we've had our share of bad luck around here lately. We've had termites in the woodwork. There've been odd accidents in the kitchen. We've had our help quitting for no reason at all. And now you get stuck in that shaft. I suppose, before we know it, the *Sea Fox* will come sailing up the Hudson River as a warning to us all."

Trixie had only been half listening to him. She was still trembling from her frightening experience, and his mournful recital wasn't making her feel any better.

All the same, she couldn't resist asking, "What's a sea fox?"

"It's a ship," Weasel said slowly, "a galleon, actually. Once it was home to a gang of pirates. Many's the time it sailed these waters when old Captain Trask was alive." He sighed heavily. "Now all that's left is a legend."

"What sort of legend?" Honey asked.

"People around here say that the old captain swore he would protect his family forever," Weasel answered. "And so, whenever something awful is about to hit one of the Trasks, his phantom galleon shows up again."

Honey peered fearfully over her shoulder at the darkening windows behind her. "A g-ghostly galleon? Are you joking?"

Weasel shook his head sadly and hurried away.

"Of course he was joking," Trixie told Honey later, as they stood, shaken, outside the entrance to the dining room. "It's the silliest story I ever heard. He probably made it up." She drew a deep breath. "I don't trust that man, Honey. I don't know why Mr. Trask keeps him on here. I know he can't help having only one eye, but at least he could shave."

Honey smiled. "He does look scary, doesn't he? All the same, he did come right away when I told him what happened."

"Why did it take so long to find somebody?" Trixie asked.

Honey frowned. "It was really strange, Trix. When I ran for help, I found most of the staff just standing around talking outside. It was as if they were waiting for something to happen." She paused. "I'm afraid there's other news, too. One of the waiters told me definitely that our dumb-waiter idea is no good. It wasn't part of the original inn. So when Captain Trask disappeared, that shaft wasn't even here. One of the later Trasks built it. Later, they bricked up the part that opened into the wine cellar, because they never used it." She stared at Trixie's face. "Hey, are you really okay? You look terrible!"

All at once, Trixie did feel terrible. After what had just happened, Honey's news was almost more than she could bear. Her knees wouldn't stop shaking, and she felt as if she didn't care anymore about vanishing pirates or ghostly galleons. Every bone in her body ached as if she had run a ten-mile race—all of it uphill.

When she and Honey reached the upstairs landing, it didn't help at all when she discovered that the other Bob-Whites had returned from their brief walk. Their cheeks were rosy, and it was obvious that they'd had a wonderful time.

Laughing and talking, they were visiting back and forth between one another's rooms.

"Tomorrow I want to explore the cliffs," Di was saying. "Tonight we walked in the other direction, but I'm simply dying to see what's beneath them. Do you suppose there's a beach?"

Mart was standing in the doorway of his "cabin." He was about to answer her when he caught sight of Trixie and Honey.

"Why the long faces, O squaws?" he sang out. "Were your exploratory perambulations unavailing?"

Trixie had been hoping to limp along the passage without causing any comment from anyone. But before Trixie could stop her, Honey had told the whole sad story of the narrow escape to five frowning Bob-Whites.

Brian, immediately concerned, pulled Trixie

inside his room. He insisted that she should stretch out full length on his bed. In an instant, she was surrounded by her worried friends.

"Are you really all right, Trix?" Jim asked, running a hand through his red hair.

"Of course she's not all right," Di said. "Look at her face. She's as white as a ghost."

"Of all the dumb things to do," Brian told Trixie sternly. "The air in that shaft could've been bad, the way it was that time when we were looking for the emerald necklace. Didn't you remember that?"

"And did you stop to think what would have happened if Honey hadn't been there to help you?" Dan added, scowling.

Wordlessly, Trixie nodded and lay stiff and quiet. Her hands, their knuckles white, were clenched at her sides.

She knew they meant well and were only concerned for her safety. All the same, the reaction from what had just happened was beginning to take effect. To her dismay, she knew that one more remark would make her burst into tears.

Strangely enough, it was Mart who came to her rescue. "Oh," he said gruffly, "leave her alone. She won't do anything like that again, will you, Trix? Besides, I've just heard a great joke I want you all to hear."

And with a graceful tact she hadn't known her brother to possess, he turned the conversation away from scoldings, and lectures, and what-might-have-beens, and instead talked firmly of other things.

Unnoticed by the others, Brian walked quietly across the room. He pulled a spare blanket from a shelf in the closet and gently placed it over her.

Trixie smiled at him gratefully and began to relax. By now, it was dark and a little foggy outside the blue-curtained windows. The golden glow from the brass lamps that hung above the two neat beds, one on each side of the room, was oddly comforting.

She could hear the leaves of the maple trees whispering softly to each other. She felt a welcome warmth from the blanket. The combination was beginning to make her drowsy.

She thought that after dinner she would read just a few chapters of her new Lucy book. Then she'd go to sleep early.

I wonder what's for dinner, anyway? she thought.

Sleepily, with her eyes half-closed, she sniffed the air to find out.

Suddenly she frowned. Her eyes flew open. All she could smell was smoke. Something was burning—and it wasn't in the kitchen!

73

The Bob-Whites turned to stare at her sharply as she leaped to her feet and ran to the door.

"Trixie?" she heard Di call. "What is it? Is something wrong?"

"Brian, Jim, Di, everyone! Hurry up!" Trixie cried. "The inn is on fire!"

It wasn't difficult to trace the source of the smoke. It billowed from beneath a closed door halfway down the hall.

Without hesitation, Dan darted ahead of the others. They heard him mutter, "The door's probably locked. We may have to break it down."

But they didn't. To their surprise, it opened to his touch. Then, with his bent arm covering his nose and mouth, he rushed inside the dark, smoke-filled room.

"One of the mattresses is smoldering!" he shouted. "Quick, Brian, Jim, Mart! Help me get it off the bed. Di, Honey! Open the windows! Trixie, we need towels to cover our faces to keep out the smoke. Hurry!"

Moments later, as Trixie raced back with as many towels as she could carry, she was just in time to see the boys stamp out the last dying embers from the mattress on the floor.

"It's all right," Dan called to her, grinning with relief. "The fire's out."

"I wonder how it got started in the first place?" Mart said, his nose smudged with soot. "It almost looks as if someone built a bonfire in the middle of the bed."

Trixie peered through the gloom and layers of smoke that still drifted lazily toward the dark, open windows. She noticed that Di and Honey had each stripped a pillow of its case. They were busily flapping them, trying to clear the air.

Trixie thought she saw something else and switched on the light. In all the excitement, no one had remembered the lights until now.

Her heart missed a beat when she realized she had not been mistaken. For a moment, she was so shocked that she couldn't have moved if her life depended on it.

As if it were a dream, she could hear the faint confusion of men's voices as they shouted to each other from another part of the inn. Then several pairs of heavy feet pounded up the stairs toward them.

Trixie looked once more at the unmoving figure on the far side of the room. Its short hair was brown. It wore a man's tan sports jacket with leather-patched elbows.

"Mart? Brian?" she said, her voice shaking. "Did someone come to help you? If not, *who's that man sitting at the desk?*"

"Man? What man?" Mart demanded, spinning around to see.

The breathless Bob-Whites stared silently as Trixie ran across the room. She gently touched the motionless figure on the shoulder.

Horrified, they watched it topple sideways and collapse in a stiff heap on the floor.

"Quick!" Honey cried. "He's probably suffering from smoke inhalation. Oh, Brian, you'll have to give him mouth-to-mouth resuscitation."

But when Brian reached the prone figure, he found out what Trixie had already discovered.

"I'm afraid," he said slowly, "that mouth-to-mouth resuscitation won't help him at all."

Mart gasped. "You mean he's—"

"I mean," Brian answered, "that our friend here would be the last one to need it. You see, he's nothing but a life-sized dummy."

Phantom From the Past • 7

JIM LOOKED BEWILDERED. "I don't believe it," he said, bending down to see the dummy's painted face. "It looks so lifelike."

"It sure does," Mart agreed, nudging it gently with the toe of his sooty sneaker. "You know, it seems to be one of those manikins you see in department stores. But what's it doing here? And whose room is this, anyway?"

No one had a chance to answer him, however, for in the next moment, Miss Trask and her brother rushed into the room. They were followed by four of the hotel staff, all of whom were wearing the now-familiar pirate costumes.

Less than a minute later, two fire fighters hurried into the room and checked the damage.

Everyone listened as Brian explained what had happened. Then Mr. Trask said, "I owe you all a debt of thanks. If you hadn't acted so quickly, there's no telling what would have happened."

"Yes," one of the fire fighters said as they went out with the remains of the mattress. "A fire in a mattress may appear to be out but actually smolder and rekindle later. These young people did a very thorough job."

Embarrassed at all the praise, the Bob-Whites couldn't think of a thing to say.

"We were glad we could help," Trixie said at last, "though when we saw the dummy—the manikin—sitting at that desk, we were shocked. We thought for a moment he was a real person."

"A manikin?" Mr. Trask said, noticing it for the first time. "Well, I'm blessed! Where on earth did that come from?"

"It's mine," a quiet voice said from the doorway. "I—er—I use him in my work. His name is Clarence." And sandy-haired Mr. Appleton, whom Trixie had last seen sitting at the captain's table, hurried into the room.

He frowned when he saw the mattress on the floor. Then Trixie saw him shoot a worried glance toward a half-opened drawer in the desk.

Before he closed it hastily, Trixie caught a glimpse of spiky handwriting covering what looked like a pad of yellow paper.

"What happened here?" Mr. Appleton asked. "And how did you all get in? This door was locked when I left this afternoon."

"It wasn't locked when we got here," Dan said slowly. "In fact, the whole incident is kind of strange."

"What do you mean, 'strange'?" Mr. Trask asked sharply.

"The fire started in the mattress," Brian explained. "There's no question about that. But the thing is, we think it was deliberately set."

Miss Trask gasped. "Oh, Brian! Are you sure?"

"Of course the boy isn't sure," her brother boomed. "How could he be? Besides, who would want to do a thing like that?"

Trixie found her gaze wandering to Mr. Appleton. He was standing with his back to the desk, almost as if he wanted to hide whatever was inside it.

"I certainly hope none of you think I had anything to do with this," he said loudly. "I haven't been anywhere near the second floor for the last three hours."

"Of course we don't think anything of the kind," Mr. Trask said.

79

All the same, Trixie thought Mr. Trask looked worried as he gave instructions to his staff to move Mr. Appleton to another room at once.

Miss Trask must have thought so, too. Only Trixie, who was standing next to her, saw her rest one hand on her brother's arm. "Do you really think it was an accident, Frank?" she asked. "I was just downstairs talking to that dreadful waiter you call Weasel. He was telling me that there's been a series of odd happenings all summer long—"

"Then you shouldn't believe everything you hear, Marge, my girl," her brother interrupted. "I'm sure this was just one of those freak things. It could have happened to anyone. Maybe it was spontaneous combustion or something."

It seemed to Trixie that Miss Trask was about to answer him sharply. Instead, she turned on her heel and hurried away.

"What was all that about, Trix?" Honey asked.

"I'm not sure," Trixie whispered. "But for right now, I'm very glad we're here. I have an idea that Miss Trask *does* need the Bob-Whites, Honey. I think there's something going on here that we know nothing about."

Mr. Appleton politely declined when first Mart, and then Jim, offered to help him move his belongings to his new room. "I can manage, thanks," he said.

He opened his closet door and threw his clothes into a suitcase. Then, after retrieving whatever was in the desk, he casually picked up the dummy from the floor. He tucked it under his arm and wandered out of the room and along the passage.

As soon as he was out of earshot, Trixie was completely overcome by an attack of giggles. "I've never seen anything so funny in my life," she gasped. "The dummy's head stuck way out in front, its legs stuck way out in back, and its body was shoved under his arm like a sack of potatoes. At any moment, I expected Mr. Appleton to use C-Clarence as a b-battering ram."

Her giggles were catching, and it wasn't long before they were all holding on to each other and shouting with laughter.

Di wiped her eyes. "It's really great to see you happy again, Trix," she said, smiling.

Trixie grinned. "And all that laughing has made me hungry. Jeepers, I'm starved!"

Jim looked ruefully at his soot-stained jeans. He sniffed at his shirt. "I hate to tell you this, gang, but I smell like a fugitive from a forest fire. I'll have to take another shower before we eat."

"I guess we all must smell pretty smoky, at

that," Mart said. "Therefore, I assume it's back to the showers for all of us. In that case, we'd better meet downstairs when we're ready." He sighed. "And let's hope that there're going to be no more worrisome adventures between now and then, okay?"

He didn't look in Trixie's direction, but she knew he meant her. The last of her giggles subsided at once, and she bit her lip.

I seem to cause nothing but trouble for everyone, she thought. *But, gleeps! I didn't start the fire. That wasn't my fault.*

"Exactly what *did* you two girls expect to find at the bottom of that dumbwaiter shaft, anyway?" Brian asked.

"I daresay Trixie was looking for Captain Trask's secret exit," Jim answered, smiling at her. "And I, for one, think it was a good idea."

Everyone knew that since Trixie had rescued Jim from his cruel stepfather, she could do no wrong as far as he was concerned.

"I hate to shatter your illusions," Mart drawled, "but I beg to differ. It was a bad idea. Figure it out for yourself. The soldiers enter the room. They're going to arrest the captain. Are you trying to tell me that from that point on, they hang back and do nothing while their prospective arrestee strolls over to a wall somewhere and disappears into the woodwork? If they had seen him do that, why didn't they follow him?''

Trixie gritted her teeth with frustration. She knew that Mart was right. It was the same argument she had used when she had been thinking of searching for a trapdoor.

She knew now that she had been too impulsive—too willing to grab the first idea that popped into her head. When would she ever learn?

"Maybe the soldiers didn't follow Captain Trask because they didn't see where he went," she answered slowly.

"Weak," Mart said, shaking his head, "very weak, Sherlock. The table's in the middle of the room, remember? How could they have *not* seen him? No, you'll have to do better than that, me hearty. Come on, Brian, I'll race you to the shower."

When everyone had gone, Trixie couldn't resist glancing around Mr. Appleton's room for one last look. Her puzzled gaze lingered on the charred mattress on the floor.

Had someone deliberately set fire to it? And had that someone been Mr. Appleton himself? It was entirely possible. After all, he had a key to the room. By why would he have done such a thing? Why would anyone?

Trixie sighed and turned to leave. As she turned, she noticed a small crumpled sheet of white paper that lay at her feet. She bent down and picked it up, then gasped as she smoothed it out and read:

BEWARE!
YOUR EVERY MOVE
IS BEING WATCHED!

"But what does it mean?" Honey cried moments later, when she and Trixie were sitting on her bed. "Is the note really meant for you, Trix? Or does it belong to Mr. Appleton?"

Trixie stared once more at the slip of paper in her hand. "I don't know, Honey," she replied. "And I don't know what to do about it, either."

"Maybe," Honey said slowly, "the best thing to do is just to keep our eyes and ears open. Surely we'll soon know if anyone is watching."

Trixie shivered and glanced quickly around the room. For the first time, she wondered if there was a secret passage somewhere in these walls, too.

She still hadn't made up her mind about it when, showered and changed once more, she stood in front of the small mirror that hung over the dressing table. Her attention slowly shifted to the unfamiliar clothes reflected in the mirror.

At the urging of Di and Honey, she had been persuaded to wear a crisp white blouse and a pretty blue skirt for the coming celebration.

"Gleeps, Honey!" she exclaimed, dragging a comb through her unruly damp curls. "You know how I hate wearing stuff like this. If Moms hadn't insisted, I wouldn't even have packed these things."

She twirled around in the center of the room until her skirt stood straight out from her waist.

"I think you always look very nice in whatever you wear," Honey said loyally. She looked very attractive herself in her pale green dress.

Trixie made one last face at her reflection. "Is Di ready?" she asked. "If so, we can go straight to the dining room and be there before the boys. They're always complaining that they have to wait for us."

But when they poked their heads into Di's room, she was not ready at all. "You go on," she said, "and I'll be with you before you know it." She paused. "You know, you two are the only ones who haven't even been outside since we arrived. You've still got time to take a quick look around. You should take your jackets, though. I think the fog's really starting to roll in now."

"That's a great idea," Trixie told Honey. "That way we can see if anyone follows us."

All the way down the stairs, Trixie had the feeling that someone's gaze was boring into her back. Twice she turned sharply, but there was no one in sight.

"I'm sure it's your imagination working overtime," Honey said.

Suddenly her grip tightened on Trixie's arm as a man's dim figure, dressed in a pirate costume, seemed to materialize in the front lobby. Quietly, almost surreptitiously, he closed a dark door behind him. Then he walked swiftly on the balls of his feet toward the dining room.

Trixie thought it was their long-faced waiter, Weasel Willis, though she couldn't be sure. And in another moment, she had forgotten the incident; she and Honey had stepped outside the front door.

Di had been right. The fog was beginning to roll in. Already it had blotted out the long stretch of grass between the inn and the cliff's edge.

Trixie shivered and pulled her Bob-White jacket tightly around her shoulders. Honey had made and embroidered jackets for all of them. Cross-stitched across the back of each were the letters *B.W.G.*, which, of course, stood for *Bob-Whites of the Glen*.

"You stay right here and watch, Honey," Trixie whispered. "I'm going to walk to the clifftop and back. In that way, we'll soon know if anyone's following me."

Honey nodded as Trixie disappeared into the fog. "Trix?" she called at last. "Are you still there? I can't see a thing."

There was no answer.

"Trixie?" Honey's voice faltered. "Where are you?"

Timidly, she began walking toward the point where she had last seen her friend. All at once, she caught her breath. Trixie was standing on the edge of the cliff. She was staring down at something that lay beneath it.

Momentarily speechless, Trixie pointed with a trembling hand. Honey stared.

Bathed in an eerie glow, its masts reaching high through the mist, was a ship. It floated silently at anchor, its sails furled. Flying from its stern was a flag that Honey strained to see.

Suddenly she clutched Trixie's arm. "Why," she cried, "the ship is a galleon, and it's flying the skull and crossbones! Oh, Trixie! Where did it come from, and why is it gleaming all over with that funny light?"

Then she read the glowing name painted on its bow—and it answered all her questions.

It was the *Sea Fox!*

A Second Disappearance · 8

REMEMBER THE LEGEND, Honey?" Trixie said at last. "The ghostly galleon is supposed to appear when disaster is about to strike the Trasks."

"B-But you didn't believe the story was t-true," Honey wailed, her teeth chattering.

"I know," Trixie answered, "and I still think there must be a logical explanation."

"Then what is it?" Honey cried. "Oh, Trix! Let's go inside. Perhaps we ought to warn Miss Trask that something awful is about to happen."

Trixie wasn't listening. Her gaze was fixed on the ship below, as if she would imprint its image on her mind forever.

She was beginning to wonder if she would see the ghastly specters of its crew come racing on deck in answer to a shouted order. Would the men then leap to the rigging and swarm up it like surefooted monkeys in a jungle's treetops?

She waited, her heart hammering against her ribs, but nothing happened. The ship appeared to be deserted.

Slowly her eyes were becoming accustomed to the ghostly light that seemed to surround the galleon. Now she could see the closed ports. She imagined the row of cannons that were probably battened down behind them.

She saw the shapely figurehead that adorned the ship's bow. The woman's graceful form appeared to be standing almost upright against the bow and was positioned just below the level of the deck.

Trixie strained to see her face and was somehow pleased when she noticed that the lady was smiling. She turned to remark on it to Honey, but the words died in her throat.

Honey was smothering a scream. In the next instant, she had clutched her friend with both hands.

Trixie turned to look. The galleon had vanished!

"But that's impossible!" she cried. "What happened, Honey?"

"I don't know!" Honey moaned. "One moment it was there, and the next it was gone. It didn't fade away or anything."

Trixie's mouth was set in a stubborn line. "I'm going down there," she said, "and I'm going to see for myself. A ship can't just vanish without leaving some sort of clue. It's impossible!"

"Oh, Trixie, please don't," Honey cried frantically. "I'm scared, and we did promise the boys we wouldn't wander off without them."

Trixie didn't remember promising anything of the sort, but she could feel Honey trembling.

"Oh, all right," she said reluctantly, allowing herself to be drawn away from the cliff's edge. "Just the same, I wish I had a flashlight—"

"The boys will never believe what we saw," Honey broke in. "In fact, no one will believe us. And what should we tell Miss Trask?"

"For the moment," Trixie said, as she hurried toward the front door, "let's not tell her anything. Our story would only worry her. Besides, nothing is going to happen tonight. I'm sure of it."

But she wouldn't have been quite so certain if she had seen a pirate's dim figure detach itself from the shadows behind them.

For a long moment, it stared after them. Then it chuckled softly.

By the time the boys arrived downstairs, the girls were already seated at the captain's table, their eyes sparkling.

In spite of her recent fright, even Honey was feeling excited. For once, the dark oak surface in front of them had been covered with a snowy white tablecloth. Polished silver had been set at each place, and, in a low bowl in the table's center, bronze chrysanthemums nodded their shaggy heads as the boys slipped into their chairs.

"Gleeps, you guys," Trixie said, pretending to smother a yawn, "we'd just about given you up. We've been waiting here for simply ages. What took you so long?"

Secretly she thought all of them looked handsome in their dark trousers and white shirts. A moment later, when Miss Trask arrived, it was obvious she thought so, too.

"Am I late?" she asked, her bright blue eyes twinkling at them. "I must say, I feel very honored to be surrounded by such a well-dressed group of young people."

"You look very nice yourself," Honey said softly as she looked at Miss Trask's plain but well-cut gray dress. "And, oh, you simply must take a sip from my glass! It's the most delicious drink you can imagine."

"Don't tell me," Mart said promptly. "Let me guess. Its name is Good-for-Your-Gullet Grog."

"Wrong!" Di chortled. "It's called Maiden's Delight!"

Gingerly, Miss Trask raised Honey's glass to her lips and sipped. "My goodness," she exclaimed, "that is good punch! What a peculiar name to give it, though. In the old days, we didn't have to think up fancy words to describe anything like that."

"And was the inn a success?" Jim asked.

Miss Trask sighed. "No, I suppose not. Oh, we had our small share of tourists during the summer. But the rest of the year, I'm afraid, things were very slow."

"Well, they're not slow now," Trixie pointed out. She looked around the crowded dining room. "The people here tonight can't be tourists, except for the Bob-Whites, that is. So it looks as if the townsfolk like it here, too."

A tall blond waiter appeared suddenly at her elbow. Although he was dressed in the usual pirate costume, he was, Trixie thought, a vast improvement over scruffy Weasel Willis, who had gloomily served them their drinks.

This waiter quickly and efficiently delivered menus to each of them. Then he grinned and said, "My name's Smiley Jackson, and when

92

you're ready, I'll take your order." He turned to Miss Trask. "The boss says to tell you he'll be joining you soon."

"I can see why he's called Smiley," Mart said when the waiter had gone. "I've never seen so many glistening bicuspids in all my life. He must have at least a hundred in his oral cavity."

Trixie laughed and studied the menu. "I almost wish Smiley had stayed and practiced some reverse psychology on us. Everything sounds so delicious, I don't know what to order."

"The Weak-Hearted Willies sound terrific," Dan said. "Listen to the description: 'Chicken pies, whose interiors will please your palate and whose exteriors will melt in your mouth.'"

"Or we could have Flaming Trask-ka-bobs," Brian said. "How does this sound? 'Chunky beef wedges, marinated in Pirate's Inn's own special and delicate sauce, skewered, and cooked to perfection over an open fire.'"

After much agonizing over the tantalizing descriptions, Smiley Jackson finally received eight orders of Captain's Chowder. The thick, creamy soup was to be followed by Swashbuckler's Steak ("cooked the way you like it"), one demure order of iced tea (for Miss Trask), three more Maiden's Delights for the girls, and four Jolly Rogers—also punch—for the boys.

Mart tried to order the Yo-Ho-Ho Rum Cake for dessert, but Smiley merely said casually, "I think the boss has something else planned for you tonight."

"Probably Yummy Yardarm Yogurt," Trixie said, jokingly, knowing her brother didn't like yogurt.

"Or perhaps I-Scream-You-Scream-We-All-Scream-for-Ice-Cream," Jim suggested.

Miss Trask sighed. "I simply don't know what to expect this evening," she said. "My brother wouldn't say what his surprise is going to be. I must say, though"—she glanced at the fearsome portrait facing her—"that picture is quite taking away my appetite."

"Would you like to change places with me?" Trixie asked quickly. "That way you won't have to look at it."

"Thank you, Trixie," Miss Trask said briskly, "but I will not be chased from my chair by an inanimate object. I can't imagine why the original painting had to be removed, though. It was much nicer than this one."

Privately, Trixie agreed with her. She wasn't sure whether this portrait really did lend atmosphere to the room. All she knew was that having it behind her made her feel acutely uncomfortable. Every time she glanced over her shoulder, she imagined that the pirate's eyes were watching only her.

When she confided this fancy to Di, she discovered that her friend had the same feeling.

"The picture isn't going to spoil my dinner," Di whispered, "but I sure wish Mr. Trask would move it someplace else. Where is he, anyway?"

When he did arrive, the Bob-Whites almost didn't recognize him. In place of his pirate chief's costume, he wore a smart dark blue suit, a pale blue shirt, and a striped tie.

Instantly, he was the courteous host, making sure that his guests had everything they wanted. Then, when they were enjoying their meal, he told them story after story of the old inn's earlier days.

Mart, not to be outdone, promptly told several stories of his own. Soon the captain's table was the merriest spot in the room.

Once, after a particularly noisy burst of laughter, Trixie found the Weasel's one eye staring in their direction. On the other hand, Mr. Appleton, who was dining alone at a small table nearby, seemed to be enjoying their conversation. On several occasions, Trixie saw him smile and lean toward them, straining to hear what was being said.

"I wonder what he's done with Clarence?" she

murmured to Honey, who immediately began to giggle again.

Trixie was having such a good time that she quite forgot to notice whether Mr. Appleton's every move was being watched—or even her own. Somehow it no longer seemed to matter. With the good food in front of her, and her laughing friends around her, she was beginning to think that she had never felt happier in her life.

At last the Bob-Whites leaned back in their chairs, wondering if their stomachs would ever be able to hold another morsel of food.

Mart groaned as Smiley Jackson deftly removed his dinner plate. "That was one of the most scrumptious meals I've ever had," he announced. "Undoubtedly, my avoirdupois has now been augmented by countless pounds and ounces."

"If that means you shoveled food into your mouth without even pausing for breath tonight," Trixie remarked thoughtlessly, "then I guess we'll all agree."

Instantly, Mart drawled, "Take care, sister dear, for your accusation could apply equally to yourself. In other words, it's merely a case of the pot calling the kettle black."

"I don't even know what you're talking about,

Mart Belden," Trixie retorted, her cheeks burning hotly.

"It means," Mart said, in his most infuriating tone of voice, "that people who live in glass houses shouldn't throw stones."

Trixie's fingers curled around the stem of her water glass as she glared across the table at her brother.

"On the other hand," Miss Trask said suddenly, "a rolling stone gathers no moss, a stitch in time saves nine—"

"And every cloud has a silver lining," Frank Trask boomed. "By gum, Marge, I'd quite forgotten that old game we used to play."

"What old game?" Jim asked, bewildered.

"When I was just a sprout, like yourselves," Mr. Trask replied, "my sisters and I used to squabble among ourselves, as youngsters sometimes do." He didn't look at Trixie and Mart. "When that happened, we often said more than we meant to. And often tempers got hot. So to cool 'em down, we used to quote old proverbs—old sayings—at each other until someone laughed, and then the quarrel was forgotten. It was our way of counting to ten, y'see." He leaned toward his sister. "We should have remembered our game the last time you were here, Marge."

Miss Trask nodded. "Yes, Frank, perhaps we

97

should have done just that." Trixie noticed that her cheeks were suddenly flushed.

"In that case," Mart announced loudly, "I hereby affirm that it is understandable that *homo sapiens* commit erroneous actions, while deity confers absolution."

Trixie looked at him and frowned. "Does that mean we shouldn't count our blessings before they hatch?"

She was startled when everyone laughed, until she noticed that Mart was laughing, too.

"You've won the game, Trix," Brian told her, grinning, "and it took you exactly one second to do it. Mart was saying that to err is human, to forgive divine."

"But it's *chickens* that shouldn't be counted," Jim explained.

Trixie, glad that Mart was no longer angry, joined in the laughter. "I'd sooner count blessings than chickens any day," she told her friends happily.

Mr. Trask leaned back in his chair. "And on that cheerful note, we get at last to the surprise I promised my sister. In fact, there are *two* surprises. Before I tell you what they are, I should explain that there was a time when my sisters and I thought we would have to sell this place. Naturally, we didn't want to. Ever since anyone can remember, a Trask has been at Pirate's Inn. It all seemed hopeless, until I had an idea."

"One of many," Miss Trask murmured.

"I borrowed some money from a good friend of mine named Nicholas Morgan," her brother said, "and with the loan, plus a touch of imagination"—he nodded toward his surroundings—"I can honestly say that the inn is a success."

"Is it really, Frank?" Miss Trask asked.

"It really is," her brother assured her. "By this time tomorrow, I will have paid off the loan, and this place will be ours again, free and clear. But there! I see we are about to be interrupted. To celebrate your presence here tonight, our chef has baked us a three-tiered cake, which"—he looked toward the kitchen—"is even now on its way to our table."

Everyone turned and watched as Weasel Willis began walking toward them, bearing their dessert on a tray.

What a cake it was! Even from a distance, the Bob-Whites could see that it was cunningly decorated with tiny anchors, minute seashells, and impudent sea gulls that rode waves of creamy frosting. Trixie nudged Honey when she saw a miniature galleon adorning the top layer.

"Do you think it's supposed to be Captain Trask's *Sea Fox?*" Trixie whispered.

Honey had no time to answer.

"Cookie—our chef—has spent hours on this, his *pièce de résistance*," Mr. Trask announced, enjoying their awed expressions. "But that isn't all! I have an announcement to make, and it's the first surprise." He paused. "*I know how the old captain disappeared!*"

Trixie's eyes were round as she stared at him. "Oh, Mr. Trask! Do you really?"

"I do, indeed." He grinned. "I figured it out early this evening. I went to an old closet in my office to hang up my costume—and I suddenly realized what the solution had to be. After all these years, it's the only possible answer."

The Bob-Whites were listening, fascinated.

"How *did* the captain disappear?" Dan asked.

"It was really very simple," Mr. Trask said. "As you know, the soldiers arrived and marched up to the captain's table—this table. They surrounded it. Then the captain merely—"

Suddenly, from somewhere behind them, came the sound of a large, heavy tray crashing to the floor. Startled, everyone swung around to see what had happened.

Across the room, Weasel Willis was gazing in horror at what lay at his feet. The beautiful cake, which had taken so many hours to make, lay smashed on the thick red carpet.

Mart groaned. "Gleeps! What a catastrophe! Maybe we ought to offer our assistance."

Trixie heard Miss Trask say sharply, "I knew you should have dismissed that waiter, Frank."

Out of the corner of her eye, Trixie saw a sudden movement. But when she turned back to look, all she saw were the other diners staring in Weasel's direction and other waiters hurrying to help him. She also saw Mr. Trask's chair pushed back from the table—but there was no sign of him in the room at all.

Their host had disappeared!

New Worry · 9

IN THE EXCITEMENT that followed, there was so much confusion that no one but Trixie had noticed that Mr. Trask was no longer with them.

As the rest of the Bob-Whites watched, the door to the kitchen swung open, and a short, dark-haired man rushed into the dining room. He wore white trousers, white tunic, and a tall chef's hat. His waxed mustache was bristling with rage.

He stared down in disbelief at his ruined creation. "You are the one great clumsy ox!" he shouted at Weasel. "For the waiter to trip over his own feet, this is unforgivable!"

"Calm down, Gaston," Weasel said, mopping vainly at the sticky mess with a damp cloth. "It was an accident. It could have happened to anyone."

"It could only have happened to you," the chef snapped, almost dancing with anger. "If you would not wear the stupid eye patch, you would have seen where you were going."

"Oh, for heavens sake," Brian muttered, "the poor guy can't help having bad eyesight."

Trixie turned her head and was just in time to see Gaston snap his fingers at the three men standing behind him. They were obviously his kitchen staff. Although they also wore white caps and aprons, Trixie could see the brightly striped T-shirts and black trousers beneath them.

Honey had an additional concern. "I noticed that Smiley hurried back to the kitchen a few moments ago," she told Trixie. "I'm sure he's gone to get us more dessert. I'm sorry about the cake, but I'm not sure I can manage anything at all. How about you?"

But Trixie was still puzzling over Mr. Trask's empty chair. "He vanished, Honey," she said slowly. "I don't know how he did it, but he's gone!"

"Who's gone?" Mart asked over his shoulder.

Trixie waved a hand at the place where, only

minutes before, their host had sat. "He said he knew the solution to the mystery of the captain's disappearance. I think maybe he's *showing* us."

Unbelieving, the Bob-Whites turned to see.

"Wow! He's done it! He's really done it!" Jim said, excited. "But how?"

"I hardly think," Miss Trask remarked, still watching the scene on the other side of the room, "that my brother would choose to vanish at such an inconvenient time."

"But he has!" Di cried. "He really has!"

Miss Trask glanced at her brother's empty chair. She smiled at Di's enthusiasm. "He'll be back," she said confidently. "I'm sure he's merely gone to see what he can do to help over there."

Trixie was certain Miss Trask was wrong. She sat watching, her eyes bright, for their host to materialize suddenly from somewhere, like a genie out of a bottle. Where would he come from?

She couldn't resist bending down to look for him under the table, though she didn't really expect to find him there. All the same, she couldn't help feeling a pang of disappointment when all she saw was the bare floor. She turned her attention to the walls, but they, too, showed no sign of secret openings.

Trixie tried to remember what Mr. Trask had

said earlier. Was it something about his pirate chief's costume that had helped him solve the mystery? If so, what could it have been?

Trixie sighed and gave up.

Gaston, the chef, was obviously still enraged at the accident to his creation. Trixie could hear him angrily directing the mopping-up operations until all signs of the catastrophe had been removed.

He had looked twice in their direction as if he expected to see or hear some comment from his employer. In the end, however, he hurried back to his kitchen, and the door swung shut behind him.

The group at the captain's table continued to wait, but Mr. Trask didn't return. Even Smiley Jackson seemed to have deserted them.

Finally, it was the Weasel who dolefully picked his way around the crowded tables until he was standing at Miss Trask's shoulder. "After all that's happened tonight, I don't suppose anyone's got any appetite left. Not that I blame you. The chef says the chocolate eclairs are fairly good tonight, but he's probably wrong." He stood expectantly, his pencil poised once more over his pad.

But this time, he received no orders, not even from Mart.

"Our dinner was the last word in gastronomic

delectability," Mart announced loftily. "However, my unerring instincts for the proprieties tell me that we ought to wait for our host to complete his magnificent, but completely mystifying, feat of prestidigitation. He's really pulled it off. He's vanished—just like the captain."

If he hoped to impress Weasel, he was mistaken. "Oh, well," the waiter said, "wherever he is, he won't have gone far. In fact, I expect he's in his office right now, waiting to bawl me out for dropping Gaston's cake. I'll go see."

"Thank you," Miss Trask said, rising to her feet, "but I'll go myself."

"Oh, Miss Trask," Trixie said, "may I come with you? I'd really like to know how the trick was done."

"Me, too!" Mart cried.

"And don't forget me," Honey added.

In the end, their curiosity aroused, they all decided to go.

Miss Trask smiled. "I don't really believe that my brother has chosen to play hide-and-seek. But by all means, come and help me look."

Trixie noticed that Mr. Appleton seemed to be disappointed as she and the Bob-Whites hurried away. Moments later, however, she forgot him as Miss Trask pushed open a door in the tiny front lobby and switched on a light.

Trixie saw a small room with the usual dark-paneled walls and red-carpeted floor. An old-fashioned safe stood next to two wooden filing cabinets, and a big oak desk was positioned under the leaded windows. Its chair, however, was as empty as the one in the dining room.

In a far corner, Trixie saw a small closet. She gazed at it expectantly. She half expected Mr. Trask to fling open its door and yell, "Surprise!"

Miss Trask must have had the same idea. Striding across the room, she opened it. To Trixie's disappointment, all it contained was the pirate chief's costume dangling from a hanger.

Trixie stared at it, hoping it would give her a clue—but it didn't.

She turned away as Weasel Willis poked his head into the room. "Did you find the boss?" he asked. "No? That's funny. He's not in his room or in the kitchen, either. It would be just our luck if he's really vanished."

"Nonsense!" Miss Trask said briskly as she sat down at the desk. "He must be here somewhere. Perhaps he's in the wine cellar."

"Maybe you'd like us to clear out of your way," Brian told Miss Trask after Weasel had gone to make another search.

She wasn't listening. She was gazing around the room as if she were remembering long-ago days when she was small. Had this once been her father's office? Trixie wondered. Had she once been bounced on his knee at this very desk?

A few minutes later, Trixie's thoughts were interrupted when Weasel tapped on the door and walked in once more.

"I've searched everywhere," he said flatly. "He's not in the wine cellar or the laundry room. I've been looking for him because we've got troubles in the kitchen."

Miss Trask hesitated. Then she said, "Very well, I'll come myself."

"You do not need to depart anywhere, Miss Trask," a loud voice said from the doorway, and Gaston marched into the room.

With a dramatic sweep of his hand, he whipped his chef's hat from his head and flung it on the desk.

"I look for Monsieur Trask," he announced, "but him I cannot find. So I tell his sister. It is this. I quit! This job is driving me oranges!"

Weasel muffled a snicker. "I think you mean *bananas.*"

He was ignored. "My cherry tart," Gaston said, "she is *très bonne, très magnifique*—the best in all of the United States. On this everyone agrees. And what am I demanded to call it? The Cannonball Pie! Pah! My assistant chefs, they have to wear the oh-so-ugly pirate costume. Pah, again! And now this man, this clumsy Weasel, who calls himself a waiter, drops my beautiful cake on the carpet, *plop!* And so I say enough is too much! Tonight I leave! Give me please my wages. I wish to leave the Pirate Inn forever."

"I told you we had troubles," Weasel murmured, sounding almost glad that he had been proved right.

There was silence. Then Mart turned to Gaston. "Please, sir, surely matters can't be that bad. Without you, the inn would not be the success it is. Your marvelous cooking brings everyone here."

"This is true," Gaston said simply. "I am, without the doubt, one of the world's best chefs. For this, I am paid much money by Monsieur Trask, who is sometimes, though not always, a shrewd man. But even for him I will not stay. You will tell him, please, that Gaston Gabriel is packing his bags. My money I will have now!"

Miss Trask did her best to persuade him to change his mind, but Gaston wouldn't listen.

"Very well, then," she said slowly at last. "We can't, of course, force you to stay against your will. But as for your salary, I'm afraid you'll have to wait until my brother returns. The money is in the safe, and I don't know its combination anymore."

Gaston tried to argue with her, but Miss Trask merely continued to smile and shake her head.

When the chef had gone, Weasel Willis intoned, "Good, very good, Miss Trask. The boss couldn't have handled that situation any better himself. Cookie's temper never lasts long, you know. In fact, this is the third time this month he's handed in his notice. But making him wait for his money was a good idea. Your brother never locks the safe these days, but Cookie doesn't know that."

Miss Trask looked startled. "Doesn't lock the safe? He *has* to lock it. There must be thousands of dollars in it!"

She rose to her feet and hurried across the room. The Bob-Whites saw her hesitate for one long moment as she knelt on the floor beside the safe. Then they saw that it opened at once to her touch. They also saw that its shelves were bare.

The money, like its owner, was gone.

A Fruitless Search · 10

MISS TRASK'S FACE was white as she rose slowly to her feet. "I simply don't understand it," she exclaimed. "The money should be here."

"I guess it still would be if we hadn't had that attempted robbery last month," Weasel remarked.

Trixie drew in her breath sharply. "What attempted robbery?"

"I told you we'd had troubles," Weasel said. "This one started late one night when everyone had gone to bed. The boss's bedroom is directly over this room, and around two o'clock in the morning, he thought he heard someone moving around down here."

"Who was it?" Brian asked.

Weasel rasped a thoughtful thumb across the stubble of his beard. "He never did find out," he said. "By the time he got down here, whoever it was had gone. But there had been a prowler, because when he looked in here, he found that someone had tried to jimmy open the safe. You can still see the scratch marks on the door. If the fool had just thought to try the handle, he could have saved himself lots of trouble."

"Did my brother call the police?" Miss Trask asked sharply.

"Nope," Weasel replied. "I told him that he should, but no one ever listens to me. He questioned the staff, o' course, but"—he shrugged— "it coulda been one of the guests, too. And he couldn't very well say much to them, could he?"

"So what did he do then?" Trixie asked.

Weasel shrugged again. "He didn't do anything. He said nothing was taken, so there was no point in making a fuss. But after that, he was more careful. Don't worry; he's probably got his cash stashed somewhere else by now." He moved toward the door. "Do you want me to keep looking for him? We probably won't get too many more for dinner tonight, anyway."

Miss Trask nodded, but she looked worried as Weasel left the room.

"I never know whether we ought to believe the stories he tells," Jim remarked.

"All the same," Brian said, "the attempted robbery story sounds genuine enough. It's his looks that make us distrust him."

"Maybe," Di said slowly, "it wouldn't hurt if we all searched for your brother, Miss Trask. I'm sure he's okay, but it's strange that no one can find him."

Trixie noticed that Di was careful not to voice the thought now at the forefront of their minds: What if something had gone wrong with Mr. Trask's disappearing trick? He could be lying hurt somewhere.

Or maybe, Trixie thought, *he's stuck at the bottom of a shaft, the way I was.*

She couldn't help shivering when she thought again about the story of the ghostly galleon. It appeared only when disaster was about to strike the Trasks, Weasel Willis had told them.

A cold hand seemed to clutch at the pit of her stomach. "Di's right," she said. "We all ought to search. And we mustn't give up till we find him."

Trixie and Honey were the only two Bob-Whites who had their jackets with them, so it was agreed that they would search the grounds around the inn immediately.

"Di and Dan will scout around inside," Brian told Trixie as they stood in the hotel lobby. "Mart, Jim, and I will join you outside as soon as we've grabbed our coats."

"Before you go," Trixie said, "there's something Honey and I want to tell you. We haven't had a chance before." Then she told them all about the ship they had seen and the story surrounding it.

Jim scratched his red head. "Maybe you only thought you saw a galleon," he said.

"Yeah, sometimes the light plays funny tricks with your eyes," Dan said.

"But we weren't seeing things," Trixie protested. "We could see the galleon as plainly as we can see you."

"That's right," Honey confirmed quickly. "The only difference was that it was—well, it was sort of gleaming all over."

"And was it made out of candy and called *The Good Ship Lollipop?*" Mart asked, grinning. "If you ask me, it sounds like the bad plot of one of Lucy Snodgrass's adventure stories."

"Or one of Cosmo McNaught's science-fiction yarns," Brian drawled in warning.

Mart flushed. "Wait till we get outside," he mumbled, "and we can see this spooky vessel for ourselves."

114

"It's not there anymore," Trixie blurted. "It disappeared."

Mart stuck his hands in his pockets and rocked gently on his heels. "I take it back," he said, gazing innocently at the ceiling. "The girls didn't get this idea from a book. They've merely had too many Maiden's Delights!"

"I should have known they wouldn't believe us!" Trixie said angrily as she and Honey hurried out the front door. "Maybe we shouldn't have told them. All the same, I've got a funny feeling that we haven't seen or heard the last of the ghostly galleon."

"Oh, Trix," Honey whispered, "I hope you're wrong!"

It was still so foggy outside that it was difficult to see anything beyond the immediate vicinity of the inn. From somewhere upriver, they could hear the mournful groaning of a foghorn. It sounded the same two notes over and over at regular intervals. It reminded Trixie of a broken record. *GER-umm! GER-umm! GER- umm!*

By the time Mart, Brian, and Jim had joined them, the two girls had already peered behind bushes and tapped outside walls, looking for clues they never found.

"What about that picnic area?" Brian said, pointing to an area just visible a little way from

115

the inn. "Did you look there? Mart, you search around the corner. Jim and I will explore the back of the place."

"I wonder what luck Dan and Di are having," Trixie muttered, feeling foolish as she peered under a redwood table.

"Have you lost something?" a man's voice asked suddenly behind them. "Do you need any help?"

Trixie spun around and saw a tall, gray-haired man watching them. She knew he must be wearing a dark suit of some kind, because all she could see of it was his gleaming white shirt front. His shoes, too, seemed to glimmer with some strange kind of polish. Then he stepped forward into a misty strip of light cast by one of the inn's windows, and she saw that his well-cut business suit was a very dark gray, and his shoes were just plain black ones, after all.

"I didn't mean to startle you," he said. "It merely looked as if you could use a hand. Did you lose a kittycat?"

"No, we were looking for someone," Honey said, before Trixie could stop her.

The man looked surprised. "Oh, I didn't realize you kids were playing a game."

"But it isn't a game," Honey cried. "You see, a friend of ours was showing us a disappearing trick. He was just about to say how it was done when he van—" She broke off as Trixie poked her sharply in the ribs.

"Vanished?" The man stepped closer to them. "Were you going to say your friend vanished?"

"Of course not," Trixie said quickly. "You were right. We're just playing a game."

The man began to turn away. Then he said, "Are you by any chance part of the group who came with Marge Trask? Ah, I thought so. I'm an old friend of hers. Frank told me you were arriving today. My name's Morgan. Nicholas Morgan. Well, goodnight, young ladies. I sure hope you win your game—whatever it is."

When he had gone, Honey said, "Why didn't you let me tell him what happened? He might have been able to help us."

Trixie frowned. "I have a feeling that we shouldn't tell anyone—at least, not yet." She sat down suddenly on a picnic bench and looked up at her friend. "Have you stopped to think what will happen if neither Mr. Trask nor his money turns up?"

Honey shivered. "Come on, Trix. Let's not think of things like that till we have to."

Trixie sighed as she and Honey hurried toward the cliffs once more and stared down into the mist below.

"I still think we ought to climb down and see what's there," she said slowly. "I simply don't believe a ship can just vanish the way that one did. Anyway, suppose there's some sort of hidden tunnel that leads from the inn to whatever is down there."

"But we could break our necks trying to climb down there in this fog," Honey protested.

So, for the second time that evening, Trixie allowed herself to be drawn away toward the inn.

"All the same," she said, "I still think my idea of a secret tunnel is a good one." Then, as they reached the picnic area once more, her thoughts returned to the man they had met there. "You know, Honey, there was something funny about him, but I don't know what it was. I wonder what he was doing here, anyway. I'm sure he's the man who lent Mr. Trask all that money."

Honey couldn't help smiling. "Maybe he's here to get some dinner before the dining room closes for the night," she replied. "Honestly, Trix, don't find any more mysteries for us to solve. I don't think I could stand it."

It wasn't long before Trixie reluctantly had to admit that she was ready to give up. "It's so foggy out here that I wouldn't be able to see a clue if one came up and bit me on the nose," she complained.

Honey began giggling uncontrollably. "I c-can't imagine a c-clue with teeth," she gasped, shaking with laughter. "That's the funniest thing I've ever heard—"

"The funny thing is," Mart said, coming up behind them, "that several of these trees around here have spotlights in them. I noticed them as soon as I got outside. And I even found the switches that are supposed to turn them on, but the dumb things don't seem to be working."

"What's not working?" Brian asked as he and Jim came hurrying toward them.

Mart explained and then added, "I kept clicking the switch off and on a while ago, but nothing happened. If I'd been able to make them work, they might have thrown some light on a dark subject. Joke! Get it?"

Brian didn't laugh. "I got it, but you can keep it, because Jim and I didn't find anything, either."

"Let's hope Di and Dan have had more luck than we have," Jim said.

When the Bob-Whites met at the dining room entrance and compared notes, however, they all had to admit they'd had no luck at all.

"You wouldn't believe the places we looked," said Di, who had a smudge of dust on her pretty nose, "but there isn't a sign of Mr. Trask."

"I even went to the garage at the back and

checked to see if his car was there," Dan said. "It *is* there, and the hood is stone cold, so he hasn't used it recently."

"Hey, that was using your old cerebrum," Mart said. "I didn't think of doing that."

"Miss Trask came and helped us," Di said. "She even took us up to the attic. But there was nothing there except the usual stuff—old lamps and things like that."

"Where is Miss Trask now?" Trixie asked.

Di stepped out of the doorway. "She's in the dining room, talking to that gray-haired man who seems to be a friend of hers. His name's Nicholas Morgan."

"Honey and I met him outside," Trixie said slowly, watching as Smiley Jackson served coffee to the pair at the table. "Honey and I think he's the man Mr. Trask owes all that money to."

"Speaking of money," Dan said, "it's still missing. We helped Miss Trask search for it, too, but it didn't turn up, either."

"I'm afraid that's not all," Di said. "Some of the waiters have got the idea that there isn't any money to find."

"But there must be," Trixie cried. "Mr. Trask said he was ready to pay back what he borrowed from Mr. Morgan. I heard him say he had the money, all in cash."

"When did you hear that?" Brian asked her sharply.

Trixie flushed and told them about the conversation she had overheard while she was stuck in the dumbwaiter shaft.

"And that was when Mr. Trask told his sister he was ready to pay back the money tomorrow night," she finished. "So it just has to be here somewhere. Even Miss Trask thought it had to be thousands of dollars."

The Bob-Whites stared at her.

"Are you certain about this, Trix?" Jim asked at last.

"I'm certain," Trixie answered.

All at once, however, she wasn't certain at all.

Midnight Mission · 11

IT WAS ALMOST MIDNIGHT when the Bob-Whites wearily decided there was nothing more they could do that night. Even Miss Trask urged them to go to bed.

"I've just been talking with Smiley, that nice young man who waited on us tonight," she told them as she sat in her brother's office chair. "I admit it sounds strange, but Smiley is convinced that my brother is playing some kind of joke on us. He's sure Frank will suddenly reappear tomorrow morning when we least expect it."

"But that doesn't make sense," Jim said, rubbing his freckled nose thoughtfully. "Why would

Mr. Trask do a thing like that?"

"Frank did say he had two surprises for us," Miss Trask reminded him. "One was that he had discovered how the captain disappeared. The other must have been—"

"To show us how it was done?" Honey asked.

Miss Trask sighed. "I confess I can't think of any other explanation. So the only thing we can do now is wait to see what happens tomorrow."

Reluctantly, the Bob-Whites climbed the stairs to their rooms.

Jim stopped at Trixie's door. "Don't worry," he told her. "It's all going to work out okay."

All the same, Trixie's thoughts were in a turmoil as she watched Honey get ready for bed. So much had happened since their arrival at Pirate's Inn. She had been trapped at the bottom of a dumbwaiter shaft. She had heard the legend of the ghostly galleon. Later, she had seen the mysterious ship with her own eyes.

As if that weren't enough, a strange fire had been deliberately set in one of the guest rooms. Trixie had received a warning that she was being watched. Mr. Trask had disappeared as completely as if he had vanished from the face of the earth. And now a large sum of money was missing. Or was it?

Trixie had noticed that Miss Trask had not

123

repeated the rumor that there was little money to find. Had she or hadn't she believed it?

"Trix," Honey asked her, emerging from the bathroom after brushing her teeth, "aren't you going to turn in? I'm so tired that I don't think I can keep my eyes open another second."

Trixie, however, was still fully dressed in her blouse and skirt. She was staring out at the fog. "You know, Honey," she said, "I sure wish my father were here."

"Why, Trixie," Honey exclaimed, "I've never known you to be homesick before."

Trixie turned her head and smiled. "No, it isn't what you think. It's just that my dad knows everything there is to know about lending and borrowing money. If he were here, he could tell me about it."

Di, toothbrush in hand, poked her head into the room. "Maybe I can help," she said. "What do you want to know?"

Trixie thought for a moment, then said, "I was wondering what would happen if Mr. Trask really didn't have the money he borrowed."

Di frowned and leaned against the door. "That's funny," she answered. "I was just thinking about that myself. I heard my parents talking about something like this once. I'm not sure if I can explain it, but I think the way it works is this:

If you want to borrow money, you usually have to give something to the lender to let him know you're going to pay him back."

"What kind of something?" Honey asked.

"I think it has to be something else of value that you own," Di said slowly. "It's called collateral, or security, or something. Then, if you can't pay back what you've borrowed, you have to forfeit whatever the thing was you'd given the lender."

"Such as the deed to this place?" Trixie asked.

Di nodded.

"So if Mr. Trask borrowed money from Mr. Morgan," Trixie said, thinking hard, "and then couldn't pay him back—"

"Then Mr. Morgan would take over Pirate's Inn." Di frowned. "Did you understand all that? I'm not sure I understand it myself."

"You made it as clear as anything," Honey said loyally.

Di looked pleased as she said good-night and went to her room.

"So that's one mystery solved," Trixie remarked.

Honey chuckled as she climbed into the lower bunk. "I know another mystery you can solve right now," she said. "You can tell me when you're going to turn out the light and get to bed."

Trixie wasn't listening. "I've just thought of

125

something else," she said. "If Mr. Trask didn't really have the money he said he did, maybe he'd try to get it."

Honey yawned. "Maybe he would."

"Then just maybe"—Trixie sounded eager—"when we were all in the dining room, he suddenly saw someone—or maybe he thought of someone—he could borrow the money from. He went to talk to him. Perhaps he thought he'd only be gone a few minutes."

"Then why didn't he say something to his sister?" Honey asked reasonably. "And why didn't he come back?"

"He didn't tell his sister," Trixie said slowly, "because he's been trying to prove to her that he's a success at last. I think, Honey, that he's had lots of ideas over the years that haven't worked out. Maybe they've quarreled about this before. And he didn't come back tonight because—" She stopped.

"Go on."

"I don't know that I can," Trixie confessed. "It all sounds so silly when I try to explain it. I was going to say that maybe the person he wanted to borrow the money from lived a long way away. So Mr. Trask got into his friend's car and—"

"You're right, Trixie," Honey told her. "When you put it like that, it does sound peculiar. I think there must be some other explanation. I can't imagine what it is, though. Let's sleep on it, okay?" She pulled the covers up to her chin and closed her eyes.

A little while later, Trixie lay in the upper bunk, staring up at the ceiling. She had tossed and turned. She had counted sheep and tried not to think about groaning foghorns, and ghostly galleons, and villainous-looking pirates—but it hadn't worked. No matter how hard she tried, she couldn't get to sleep. Her brain was still too busy trying to solve the mystery of Mr. Trask's disappearing trick.

Moving quietly, so as not to disturb Honey, who was breathing deeply, Trixie sighed and gave up. She switched on the little brass lamp over her head. Then she reached for her new Lucy Radcliffe novel, *Mission in Munich*, and opened it to the first page.

She read:

Chapter One

I was in danger. I knew it as soon as I moved to the head of the stairs. I should have sensed it sooner. After all, I had just found my partner bound and gagged in the musty linen closet on the second floor. Now he was powerless, and it was up to me to save us both.

I paused with my hand on the banister rail and

listened. Someone—or was it some*thing?*—was moving about in the darkness below!

I could see my reflection in the mirror that hung on the wall beside me. A tall, slim girl, about eighteen years of age, with dark red hair and wide green eyes, stared back at me. Her complexion was flawless. Her long, golden dress hung gracefully from her white shoulders.

"Easy now, Lucy," I whispered to her. "The fate of your country depends on your next move."

Trixie sighed contentedly and settled herself into a more comfortable position against her pillow. "So much for Mart!" she muttered under her breath. "Lucy doesn't either have zits!"

She read on:

All at once, as I peered through the gloom, I heard a door open softly. A man's caped figure appeared suddenly before me. And the secret plans that I had been sent to Germany to defend with my life were tucked firmly under his arm.

Trixie gasped and sat up, almost bumping her head on the ceiling.

Lucy was not the only one to have seen a dim figure emerging from a doorway. Trixie, too, had seen the same thing earlier that evening. Why had she forgotten about it until now? Trixie and Honey had been coming down the stairs into darkness, just as Lucy Radcliffe had.

Trixie hadn't seen a caped figure, however. She had seen a pirate. He had been hurrying out of a room that Trixie now knew was Mr. Trask's office. Who was he, and what had he been doing there?

She kicked off the covers and hung way over the edge of the top bunk. "Honey!" she cried. "You've got to wake up! I've just thought of something else. Suppose Mr. Trask *did* have the money, after all. And suppose he had it hidden somewhere in his office. Someone could be trying to find it!"

Honey grunted and gazed bleary-eyed at the upside-down face dangling in front of hers. "Go to sleep, Trix," she mumbled. "We'll talk about it tomorrow."

"But I want you to wake up," Trixie insisted stubbornly. "This could be important. Earlier this evening, we saw someone sneaking out of Mr. Trask's office, remember? Who was it?"

Honey tried to blink the sleep out of her eyes. "I don't know," she said at last. "I didn't get a good look."

Trixie jumped to the floor and reached for her clothes. "If I'm right," she said excitedly, pulling on her jeans and warm turtleneck sweater, "then whoever it was could be trying to cause trouble for the Trasks. I think the would-be thief could have been the one who set the fire, too."

Honey leaned up on one elbow. "But where are you going, and what're you going to do?"

Trixie picked up her Bob-White jacket from the chair and threw it around her shoulders. "There may be a clue right now in that office. Besides, if the money is there, we ought to find it before someone else does. Anyway, I'm going to look."

"Now?" Honey wailed. "You're going to look *now?*"

"Oh, Honey," Trixie answered, "don't you see? Tomorrow may be too late."

It didn't take Honey long to dress, but she was still arguing as she and Trixie began tiptoeing silently down the stairs.

"I don't know why I let you talk me into this," she whispered. "We've already looked everywhere in that room once tonight, and we didn't find anything. Oh, please, let's go back to bed."

"Lucy Radcliffe wouldn't go back to bed," Trixie replied obstinately. "She would just toss her gorgeous red hair back from her face, set her jaw firmly, and stick at it until the case was solved. Jeepers, Honey! How I wish I were a spy. Lucy leads such an exciting life."

130

Honey tried to smother a yawn. "Then Lucy can have it," she declared. "Everyone else is asleep, and I wish I were, too."

They had almost reached the bottom of the stairs when they stopped to listen. Around them, the inn was quiet and still. The polished brass ship's lanterns, which hung at intervals along the walls, cast soft light and shadows on the stair treads beneath their feet.

Now that they were close to the mysterious dining room, Trixie thought she could smell the familiar fragrances of fresh-baked fruit pies and newly risen bread dough.

"If I close my eyes," she whispered, "I can almost believe I'm back in our kitchen at Crabapple Farm."

"If I close my eyes," Honey retorted, "I can almost believe I'm back in the bottom bunk in our room at Pirate's Inn—where I belong!"

Trixie grinned and paused on the last step. The dimly lit lobby was in front of them. Then, as she was about to hurry across it, she heard someone moving on the other side of the office door. She heard the soft click of a light switch.

Motioning Honey to silence, Trixie pressed herself against the wall and waited.

The doorknob turned without a sound, and a tall, skinny figure appeared in the opening.

The man wore a red scarf around his head, and a black patch over one eye. A stubble of gray beard covered his chin.

This time there was no doubt at all about his identity. The man was Weasel Willis.

Then Trixie's heart skipped a beat when she saw what he was carrying in his hands.

It was a large metal cashbox.

The Crying Lady · 12

IN THE NEXT MOMENT, everything seemed to happen at once.

In spite of Trixie's warning, Honey took a quick step forward. She put out a hand, as if to stop him. Startled, Weasel looked up and caught sight of the two girls watching from the shadow of the stairs. At almost the same instant, the door to the dining room swung open.

"Weasel?" a man's voice called. "Did you find it?" And Gaston, the chef, minus his white cap, stepped out to join them.

The sudden appearances seemed to be too much for Weasel. The cashbox dropped from his nerveless fingers. To Trixie's astonishment, a shower of golden coins cascaded to the floor in a shimmering stream.

One of them rolled to the bottom of the stairs.

Honey stared at it. "Golly," she breathed. "They're old gold coins!"

"They're golden doubloons!" Trixie exclaimed. "Jeepers! They must be worth a fortune!"

Honey, however, had just taken a closer look. "Oh, Trix," she said, "it isn't gold at all. It's—"

"—chocolate wrapped in embossed gold foil," Weasel said wearily.

Trixie was beginning to feel a little like Alice in Wonderland. Peculiar things happened to *her* all the time, too.

"Chocolate?" she echoed. "You mean this is just chocolate?" She watched, disappointed, as Honey peeled off the "coin's" outer covering.

Weasel seemed amused. "Looks real, don't it?"

Trixie said nothing as she went to help him gather up the scattered candy. Of course they weren't gold pieces. She could see that now. She couldn't imagine how she had ever thought they were.

"It is very poor chocolate, because I do not make it myself," Gaston announced grandly. "It is even worse chocolate now it has been dropped —*plop!*—on the carpet by the clumsy ox."

134

All at once, Weasel looked angry. "You'd better watch who you're calling an ox," he snapped.
"I tell you I couldn't help it. You all popped out
of the woodwork at me at once. It made me jump,
is all." He sighed. "This just hasn't been my day.
Not that it ever is."

Gaston ignored him. "Monsieur Trask, he buys
the chocolate," he explained to the girls. "He
stores it in his office for *les enfants*—the little
children—who come to the inn. They like it
because it looks like pirate money. Is it not so?"

Trixie was about to agree fervently that at first
glance it did indeed look like pirate money. Then
she saw the Weasel staring at her.

"I'll bet you thought I was about to sneak out
of here with a load of cash, eh?" he said. "But the
cashbox is just for effect, y'see. It's kept in the
dining room by the cash register."

Trixie felt her face grow hot. But before she
could answer, Honey said, "We didn't think you
were sneaking off with anything, Mr. Willis."

"Of course not," Trixie said quickly. She
glanced longingly at the office. She and Honey
would have to search it later. "My friend and I
couldn't sleep," she added, "so we thought we'd
get a breath of fresh air instead."

Gaston frowned. "It is very late for two young
ladies to be taking the fresh air," he declared. "It

135

is even late for the Weasel and myself to be working. But in the absence of Monsieur Trask, we have to prepare for the morning customers. But you girls should be getting the sleep of beauty."

"My friend doesn't need beauty sleep," Trixie said hastily, pulling Honey toward the front door. "Anyway, we won't be gone long. We're sorry we startled you, Mr. Willis. Good night."

A moment later, they stood on the top step, with the fog swirling around them once more.

"We lied, Trix," Honey said. "We did think they were stealing—at least, I did."

"I did, too," Trixie replied, "but we couldn't very well tell them so."

Honey shivered. "How come they're inside, where we want to be, and we're outside, where it's cold and damp?"

Trixie squeezed her friend's arm. "I'm sorry. I told them the first dumb thing that came into my head." She sighed. "I suppose I shouldn't have waked you up at all."

"Of course you should," Honey declared. "I'd never have forgiven you if you'd wandered off without me." All the same, Trixie saw her trying hard to stifle another yawn.

"We'll just wait for a couple of minutes until Gaston and Weasel have gone," she said, "then we'll go back inside, okay?"

"Back to bed?"

Trixie hesitated. "I guess if we can't get into the office tonight, we'll have to leave it till tomorrow," she said reluctantly.

It seemed that Gaston was still concerned about them, for the front door opened again, and he hurried toward them.

"Sometimes I am slow on the intake—" he said.

"Doesn't he mean *up*take?" Trixie whispered to Honey.

"—but I still remember when I was a boy," Gaston continued, stroking his mustache. "In those days, I liked to look at the surprises many times. And this, I tell myself, is what you have come to see again, no? For this you decide not to sleep. And this I understand now."

"Surprise?" Honey said.

"But yes! Monsieur Trask's big surprise. She is beautiful, is she not?"

Trixie frowned. "Do you mean Mr. Trask's disappearing trick?"

"Of the vanishing trick, I know nothing," he told them. "Of the ship, I know everything."

Trixie and Honey exchanged quick glances.

Gaston looked from one to the other. "But what is this? Do you tell me this is not what you have come to see?"

137

"I'm not sure we know what you mean," Honey said.

"But you do," Gaston insisted. "The Weasel, he tells me everything. He should not have spoiled the big surprise, but he showed it to you."

"I didn't know Mr. Willis showed us anything," Trixie replied, puzzled.

"But it is the galleon of which I speak," Gaston said. "The Weasel, he tells me he repeats to you the old legend. Then, before your so-magnificent dinner, he sees you walking toward the cliff. He cannot resist it. He stands right here by the front door. He flips on the lights, so!" He reached to a set of switches on the outside wall. "And *voilà!* The *Sea Fox*, she sails again."

Trixie stared through the fog toward the river, but from the inn, she could see nothing that lay below the cliff.

Honey seemed to feel as confused as Trixie. "I'm afraid I still don't understand, Mr. Gabriel," she said. "We saw the ship vanish—"

"But of course it did," Gaston said patiently. "The ship, she is being painted now with fluorescent paint. The lights, they are very special ones. They are black."

Trixie was beginning to understand. "I've seen black lights used to illuminate some aquariums," she told Honey.

"When these lights are turned on at night,"
Gaston continued, "ah, what a mystification!
The ship, she glows in the dark. When the lights
are turned off—*poof!*—the galleon, she disappears. Monsieur Trask, he did not show you
this?"

"Maybe he was going to just before he—he had
to leave," Trixie said slowly. "Oh, Mr. Gabriel,
are you sure about this?"

"But of course I am sure," Gaston answered.

"And Mr. Trask owns the ship?" Honey asked.

"Mais oui!" Gaston exclaimed. "He looked a
very long time for the pirate ship. He decided he
needed it to give the inn—"

"Atmosphere?" Trixie suggested.

"Exactly!" Gaston beamed at her. "So Monsieur Trask one day finds what he looks for. He
finds a ship which has been used on the moving
picture."

"He got it from a movie lot?" Honey asked.

"The ship, she has sailed up and down, down
and up, in the ocean," Gaston told her. "The ac-
tors and actresses, they have swooned on the
decks. They have climbed in the eagle's nest—"

"Crow's nest," Trixie murmured.

"And when the movie is finished, Monsieur
Trask, he buys this so-beautiful galleon for not
very much money, yes?"

139

Trixie was fascinated, watching Gaston as he accompanied his remarks with wide, expressive movements of his hands. "What happened then?" she asked breathlessly.

"The galleon, she is brought all the way to the Hudson River," Gaston said. "And then the workmen come. They start the work to make her look like the bad pirate boat. But the work, it is not yet finished. The ship is not yet ready to be illuminated all the time. But Monsieur Trask, he is very excited. He wishes to show his so-excellent sister how very clever he has been. This is his big surprise."

"So that was it!" Trixie was thoughtful.

"I wonder why we didn't see the ship when we first arrived this afternoon," Honey said, frowning. "I remember looking at the river, but I didn't see a galleon."

"Ah," Gaston said, "but what trouble Monsieur Trask takes to make sure that you did not. The ship, she is towed around a headland yesterday to put her in hiding. At dusk today, she is towed back."

Honey gasped. "Was that why all the kitchen staff was outside when Trixie got stuck in the dumbwaiter?"

"There are times," Gaston said, "when even grown men like to see the spectacle. Even I had

140

to see the tall ship coming home. But enough! I myself will show you again how beautiful she is. I think the fog, she is lifting a little. I will stay here. Then—click, click—I will work the lights. After this is done, you will both go quickly up the stairs to get the sleep of beauty. I know this is important for growing young ladies."

"I wonder if we ought to wake up the others?" Trixie said. "The boys would sure like to explore the ship, I know."

"But this is not possible," Gaston answered. "You will kindly remember that much work is being done on board. You will look only."

"Gosh," Honey said as she and Trixie hurried toward the edge of the cliff, "he really seemed worried about us. I sure hope he doesn't pack up and 'leave Pirate's Inn forever.' "

"Maybe Weasel was right," Trixie answered. "Perhaps he does have a quick temper and just needed time to cool down. He certainly seems in a good mood now."

They were both moving carefully when they came close to the place where they had seen the ghostly ship appear before.

The fog did seem to be lifting a little, but although they glanced up several times at the tall trees around them, they still couldn't see the spotlights Gaston had assured them were there.

"I don't know how Mart saw them in the first place," Trixie muttered. "He must have eyes like a cat. And wait till I tell him we weren't imagining things, after all."

"Too many Maiden's Delights, indeed!" Honey said, grinning.

All at once, the path in front of them seemed suddenly brighter. When the two girls looked at the river, there was the galleon, gleaming in the water.

The tall masts and the shimmering deck stood out against the night sky. Trixie saw the flag of the Jolly Roger, which, she thought, was probably lit by a special small spotlight of its own.

She saw the wooden figure that stood proudly against its bow. She looked for the happy smile that had so pleased her before.

The smile was still there—but so was something else.

To Trixie's astonishment, sorrowful tears appeared to be trickling down the painted face.

"Oh, Honey!" Trixie gasped. "It doesn't seem possible, but the lady's crying!"

Clues to a Treasure · 13

LATER, TRIXIE could imagine Gaston standing by the light switches muttering to himself, "Click, click—ah, what a mystification!—here is the ship. Click, click—*poof!*—the ship, she is gone."

True to his word, and while the girls watched, he made the galleon appear and disappear once, twice, three times.

Then, just before the ship vanished for the last time, Honey asked, "Trix? *What's that?*"

Trixie was still puzzling over the strange sight of the crying figurehead. But she tore her gaze away from the river and followed Honey's pointing finger.

She drew in her breath sharply, for what she saw on the grass where they were standing were the faint outlines of glowing footprints. They seemed to march toward the inn. In the next second, as Gaston turned off the lights, the footprints, too, vanished into the mist.

"What on earth were they?" Honey asked.

"I can think of a better question," Trixie answered. "Who or what made them?"

She still hadn't made up her mind when they joined Gaston at the inn's front door.

"The ship, she is truly astonishing, yes?" he remarked, firmly ushering them inside. "And now goodnight, *mes amies*. In the morning, Monsieur Trask, he will have returned, and all will be well."

"It's funny how everyone is so certain that Mr. Trask will come back tomorrow," Trixie said, watching him hurry away. "I only hope everyone's right!"

She glanced quickly around her, but she could see no one, not even the owner of the ghostly footprints. Who *had* made them?

The Weasel, too, was nowhere in sight. Trixie found herself hoping that he'd gone to bed. She didn't trust him at all. She had the feeling he was playing some strange game of his own.

The dining room was dark and deserted, but

the tables, or what she could see of them, had been neatly set for breakfast. The inn seemed to be functioning well, even in the absence of its owner.

Trixie couldn't help feeling a bit guilty as she moved toward the office door. She knew that Gaston had assumed that she and Honey were going straight upstairs.

It had been kind of him to solve the mystery of the vanishing galleon. On the other hand, there were still many questions left unanswered. She was sure, however, that the next few minutes would answer at least one of them.

"We'll make a real quick search until we find the missing money," she told Honey, "then we'll go to bed, okay?"

Honey was staring fearfully over her shoulder. "I keep on getting this funny feeling we're being watched," she said. "Oh, Trixie, suppose it's the same person who sent you that warning note."

Trixie swung around to face the stairs. She was just in time to see two shadows slowly descending. Then she heard familiar voices muttering, "Six, seven, eight—"

"Brian? Mart?" Trixie called, astonished. The shadows stopped.

"Trix, is that you?" Mart's voice said. In the next moment, he had run the rest of the way and

145

was facing her. He was fully dressed in jeans, shirt, and Bob-White jacket, as was Brian, who quickly joined them. The four stood staring at each other.

"What are you doing here?" Trixie demanded.

"We were about to ask you the same thing," Brian said. "We thought you'd gone to bed."

"We thought you did, too," Honey said quickly. "But wait till you hear what's happened. Trixie found out that we weren't seeing things after all. We really did see a galleon."

The boys listened as she told them all about it.

When she had finished, Brian said sternly, "I thought it was agreed that you wouldn't go wandering off without us, Trix."

"No more clandestine adventures unless we were with you," Mart added. "Though I must say, the spectral vessel does sound devastatingly tempting. If I didn't have something far more important to do, I might be persuaded to sashay up the gangplanks right now."

"You can't," Trixie said. "It's dangerous. No one's allowed on board. Gaston said so."

"I still don't understand why you two came down here in the first place," Brian said, looking from one to the other of them. "You weren't dumb enough to go looking for more secret passages, were you?"

146

Trixie's cheeks were crimson as she told her brothers how convinced she was that the missing money was in the office. Now that she was explaining her theory, she could tell how weak it sounded. It was based on nothing but a hunch.

"Well, the money isn't there," Brian told her flatly. "Miss Trask searched for it, and later, so did Di and Dan. I'm beginning to think there isn't any to be found."

Trixie's face fell. "I was so sure—"

"Why don't you two go to bed," Mart said. "We'll talk about it in the morning."

Something in his voice made Trixie instantly suspicious. "You've been so busy asking us questions," she retorted, "that you still haven't told us how come you're down here, too."

"Why, Trixie," Honey exclaimed, watching their faces, "you're right! They're up to something, as sure as my name's Honey Wheeler. Okay, you two—confess."

Reluctantly, Mart pulled a piece of paper out of his pocket and unfolded it. "I found this tucked away in a secret drawer in the desk in our room," he said. "I'll bet it's been there for years. Brian and I were just going to see what we could find, that's all."

When Trixie took the yellowed paper from his hand, she could see that it was covered with spidery handwriting. The ink looked faded, as if it had been written long ago.

Astonished, Trixie read aloud:

> "Thirteen paces down the stair,
> Then through the door—
> Soon you'll be there,
> Where fortune waits upon the shore,
> Inside a cave, upon the floor.
> Beware of ghosts who guard the place
> With knife and cutlass, gun and mace.
> Faint heart ne'er did a rich man make,
> But gold is there for you to take.
> If you can find the pirate's lair,
> Then you have won a treasure rare."

Honey had been reading over Trixie's shoulder. "A treasure?" she gasped, her eyes wide. "You found clues to a *treasure?*"

"And you were going looking for it without telling us?" Trixie glared at her brothers.

Mart shuffled his feet. "We thought you were asleep," he mumbled. "Besides, it might not be anything at all."

"But it's as good as a treasure map," Trixie cried.

"All right," Brian said, sighing, "you can come with us if you want to."

Honey hesitated. "Shouldn't we wake up Di and Dan and Jim?"

"We were wondering when someone would remember us," Jim's voice said. In another moment, Jim, Di, and Dan appeared, and the seven Bob-Whites were crowded in the little lobby, grinning at each other.

Dan said, "All we could hear were whispers and footsteps—"

"And doors opening and closing," Di added. "So we got up to find out where everyone was. What's going on, anyway?"

For the second time that evening, Honey told them about the galleon; then Mart related the story of his discovery. When he showed everyone the paper, each Bob-White had several questions to ask.

At last, Jim repeated thoughtfully, " 'Thirteen paces down the stair. . . .' Does it mean these stairs?"

"I think so," Brian answered. "I counted them automatically when we first went upstairs this afternoon. There are exactly thirteen of them."

"And 'Then through the door—soon you'll be there . . .' " Mart quoted, moving forward. "That must mean this door. Onward, me hearties! This way to the treasure!"

Honey sighed as she found herself once more on what she considered to be the wrong side of the door—the *out*side.

"Do you really think that we'll find treasure, Trix?" she asked, pushing her feet through the damp leaves that lay on the driveway.

"Where there were pirates, there was often treasure," Trixie pointed out. "I know that lots of it was never found. They've never discovered where Captain Kidd hid his gold, remember. Maybe Captain Trask had a secret hiding place, too."

"Did anyone bring a flashlight?" Jim asked, trying to peer through the fog.

A bright beam of light from Mart's hand answered his question.

"Over here," Mart called, leading the way across the grass. "Watch your step, everyone."

"What's the next part of the verse?" Dan asked as the rest of them caught up to Mart.

Mart shone the light onto the paper. " 'Inside a cave, upon the floor.' I sure hope there's an easy way of getting down to the beach—"

He broke off as his wavering beam unexpectedly spotlighted two figures who had appeared through the mist in front of him.

Trixie peered at them and then couldn't believe her eyes. Two men appeared to be locked in mortal combat!

She recognized the slight build of one of them at once. It was Mr. Appleton! She could hear him panting as he struggled furiously with his dark-haired opponent. She gasped as she realized that they were dangerously close to the cliff's edge.

"Hold on!" Brian shouted.

"We're coming!" Jim cried, racing forward.

Mr. Appleton turned a startled face toward them as the four boys rushed to the rescue.

But, as Trixie watched, horrified, Mr. Appleton's opponent appeared to stagger.

Before anyone could reach him, he toppled slowly forward, then plummeted straight to the beach far below.

The Cave · 14

FOR A MOMENT, the Bob-Whites were too shocked even to move.

Then Mr. Appleton said mildly, "It wasn't your fault, you know. I shouldn't have let go of him. Poor old Clarence! I hope he's not damaged." He moved to the edge and peered into the mist below.

"Clarence?" Mart sounded incredulous. "You—you mean that was just your dummy?"

"But we saw you struggling with him," Brian said, "and we thought—"

Mr. Appleton looked embarrassed as the girls hurried to join them.

"I—er—that is, Clarence and I were taking a stroll," he said.

"It didn't look like a stroll to us," Trixie pointed out. "We thought you were fighting with someone."

There was silence as the Bob-Whites realized they had only Mr. Appleton's word for it that it *was* Clarence who had fallen over the cliff.

Mr. Appleton sighed. "I suppose I'd better tell you the truth." He paused and seemed to be thinking hard. "The fact is, my hobby is wrestling, and I use Clarence in my workouts. He helps me keep in shape." He peered over the edge once more. "I can't see a sign of him. I'll have to leave him there until this fog clears off. Well, good night to you. Thanks for trying to help. I suppose the two of us did look kind of peculiar, at that." And with a friendly wave of the hand, he turned away and strolled back toward the inn.

"Wrestling, indeed!" Trixie exclaimed, when he was out of earshot. "Wrestlers have muscles. Even I have more than he has! I don't believe he was telling us the truth."

"Then what do you suppose he was up to?" Honey asked.

Brian frowned. "Aw, come on, Trix. I think you're being too suspicious. His story sounded

153

just peculiar enough to be true."

"At least we can find out about the dummy," Mart said. "If my calculations are correct, we need to go down there, anyway."

Slowly, carefully, the Bob-Whites searched for a path to take them to the beach. It wasn't long before they discovered a flight of wooden steps. Although they appeared to be old, they were in surprisingly good condition.

"If I'd known about these before," Trixie told Honey, following the others, "I'd have been able to solve the mystery of the vanishing ship all by myself."

"We didn't have Mart's flashlight to guide us before," Honey pointed out sensibly.

Trixie had to admit that the journey down the cliff might have been far more difficult in the fog without the beam of light to guide them. As it was, she was soon standing safely on the tiny beach at the bottom.

Her eyes were gradually becoming accustomed to her surroundings. Beneath her feet were small pebbles that littered the shore. To her right, a long wooden jetty, with signs forbidding anyone to enter, extended into the water. At the end of it, a dark mass floated gently in the current.

"It's the galleon!" Trixie told the others in hushed tones. "I wish we could see it better."

As if in answer to her wish, the mist lifted momentarily, and for the first time without the aid of special lights, Trixie gazed on the ship as it stood at anchor.

What a magnificent sight it was! Although it no longer glowed, Trixie thought she had never seen anything more beautiful. Immediately, her eyes searched for and found the figure at its bow.

Honey must have done so, too. She took a step forward and then frowned and said slowly, "That's funny, Trix. I thought you said the lady had tears running down her face. I can't see anything like that at all."

Trixie could see that Honey was right. "That *is* funny," she said. "I wonder how I made such a dumb mistake."

She was still thinking about it when Mart shouted, "I've found the body!" A cold hand seemed to clutch at Trixie's heart until he added, "It *is* Clarence, and he seems to be fine."

Trixie grinned when she saw Mart hurrying toward them. He was carrying Clarence over his shoulder, fireman-style. He was also carrying his flashlight in one hand, and something else in the other.

"It's Clarence's arm," Mart explained, waving it in the air. "It fell off. His nose is slightly bent out of shape, and his wig is coming unglued on

155

one side. But other than that, he's great, aren't you, Clarence, old boy?"

"I'b dot gread ad all," a gruff voice said crossly. "By dose hurts. Yours would, doo, if you'd bupped id od a rock."

"*Clarence?*" Di cried. She walked quickly behind Mart and bent down to peer at the dummy's face. "Did—did you say something?"

"Of course he didn't," Trixie answered, grinning. "It was Mart. I saw his lips move."

Mart sighed. "Ah, well, back to the drawing board. I've been practicing a ventriloquist act for the school's talent show next week. I thought I was getting pretty good."

"But not good enough to pull the wool over Trixie's sharp eyes," Jim assured him.

"I thought it was excellent, Mart," Honey said loyally. "It almost fooled me, too."

They gathered around him to read the next clues that they hoped would guide them to the treasure.

"I read what it said about the shore," Mart declared, heaving poor Clarence to a more comfortable position. "The next bit says, 'Beware of ghosts who guard the place. . . .' "

" 'With knife and cutlass, gun and mace.' " Dan was reading over Mart's shoulder.

"What's a mace?" Di asked.

"It's a long stick with a spiked iron ball on the end of it," Brian told her.

Di shuddered.

" 'Faint heart ne'er did a rich man make,' " Mart continued, " 'but gold is there for you to take. If you can find the pirate's lair, then you have won a treasure rare.' " He looked at the circle of faces around him. "Now all we have to do is find the cave. Right, Clarence?"

"You're always right, Mart," the gruff voice answered. "In fact, with your omniscient and magnificent intellect, how could you ever be anything else?"

"I wish you wouldn't do that, Mart," Trixie snapped, suddenly nervous. "Oh, I wish we'd never come down here at all. I've got a feeling something terrible's about to happen."

Honey squeezed her arm. "Hey, Trix, if you really want to go back up, I'll go with you."

"Me, too," Di said quickly. "I wish I'd never asked what a mace was. I know I wanted to see the beach, but"—she looked over her shoulder—"I'd rather see it in daylight."

"You'd never see your way back up the cliff without us," Brian said. "If you want to, though, we'll leave you here while we explore."

"No," Trixie said. "I think that we should all stick together, no matter what."

157

As they moved away from the jetty, the fog closed in around them once more. Soon a pile of jagged rocks loomed beside them.

"I found Clarence right here," Mart announced, pointing to one of them. "It's a wonder he didn't crack up." He gave the dummy a friendly thump on the leg. "Plastic," he explained. "It's a good thing, too—for his sake."

Brian took the flashlight from Mart's hand. He played the beam of light over the rocks and then toward the base of the tall cliffs behind them.

"I was right!" he cried suddenly. "I thought I saw an opening. Look, there it is! It's Captain Trask's secret cave!"

" 'Faint heart ne'er did a rich man'—or woman—'make,' " Mart yelled. "So come on, you guys! This way to the treasure."

The cave was dark and cold as the Bob-Whites stepped inside it. It had a dank, musty smell. It reminded Trixie of the dumbwaiter shaft.

She shivered as Mart, holding the flashlight once more, moved forward eagerly. "Get a move on, everyone!" he ordered. "Follow me!"

Brian, Jim, and Dan needed no second bidding. After a moment's hesitation, Honey and Di joined them.

Trixie stumbled forward, the last one to enter

the cave. She was surprised at her own reluctance. At any other time, she would have scrambled ahead of everyone else.

She couldn't help remembering, however, another cave, in which she and the Bob-Whites had been searching for ghost fish. She also remembered what had happened there.

She shivered again and crept forward, wishing the others would wait for her.

Inside, it was pitch-black. She could feel the soft sand beneath her feet. It deadened all sound of her progress.

Her groping fingers reached for the wall, but instantly she snatched her hand away as it encountered something horridly slippery. Was it a jellyfish? Trixie thought it unlikely. The cave itself appeared to be too dry for any of the river's creatures to reach it. Besides, a jellyfish lived only in salt water. Or did it? Try as she might, she couldn't remember.

"There's something about this place I don't like," she muttered to herself.

A man's deep chuckle answered her.

"Brian?" Di's voice called from somewhere ahead of her. "Was that you laughing?"

"It wasn't any of us," Jim's voice called.

Trixie hurried toward the sound of their voices and soon reached her friends. "It was Mart," she announced. "He's making that dummy talk again."

"But I didn't say anything, honest!" Mart protested, stopping dead in his tracks. "Neither did Clarence."

Trixie heard Honey take a deep, quivering breath. "But if it wasn't one of us—then *who was it?*"

In a penetrating whisper, someone said, "Beware the ghosts who guard the place—"

At that moment, the flashlight's comforting beam flickered and died, and suffocating blackness enveloped them all.

Treasure Island · 15

IF THE BOB-WHITES had been able to see where they were going, they would have immediately turned and run back the way they had come— but it was too late!

Trixie, glancing over her shoulder, could see nothing of the cave's entrance. They had come too far!

For a moment, no one said anything. Then everyone began talking at once.

"Oh, come on, you guys," Di said, her voice trembling. "A joke is a joke, but this isn't funny anymore."

"That's right!" Honey exclaimed. "Which one

of you is playing the part of the ghost? Jim, is it you?"

Jim, meanwhile, had turned to accuse Dan, who was already protesting his innocence.

"For crying out loud, Mart," Brian was saying, "you were supposed to buy new flashlight batteries."

"I did," Mart cried. "Unfortunately, I forgot to bring them with me. They're still in our room, back at the inn." He paused. "Fortunately, I've got a great idea. Maybe our friendly ghost will go get them for us. How about it, whoever you are?"

The Bob-Whites strained their ears for another sign that would tell them they were not alone, but no one answered.

"Maybe whoever it was has gone," Jim muttered, voicing the thought in everyone's mind.

"Now what do we do?" Dan asked. "We can't stay here forever. I'm going to try to find the way out of here and—"

Suddenly Trixie reached out toward the sound of Dan's voice. She put a hand on his arm. "Wait!" she whispered hoarsely. "Something's happening."

Honey groaned. "Oh, Trix!" she wailed. "Don't say that! I'm not sure I can take any more excitement."

Honey had no choice in the matter. The Bob-Whites were slowly discovering that, astonishingly, the darkness around them was lifting. Soon they could see each other's dim outlines. Then they began to notice their surroundings.

Open-mouthed, they stared around them. Now they could see that they were standing in a low-ceilinged cavern where the rough rock surfaces appeared to be green with age.

Here and there, moss seemed to cling to tiny crevices, and small fungi clustered in places along the walls.

Trixie shuddered and surreptitiously wiped her hand on her jeans. She realized it must have been this that her fingers had touched moments before. She hoped the fungus wasn't the poisonous kind.

She could also see a massive boulder that lay sprawled on its side on the sandy floor. It looked as if it had been flung there by some gigantic hand. Beyond it, the shadows were impenetrable.

Mart hefted Clarence to a more comfortable position on his shoulder. Then he gripped the dismembered arm by its wrist. He raised it slowly over his head as if to use it as a weapon. If they hadn't been so apprehensive about what might happen next, the Bob-Whites would have laughed.

As it was, Mart said grimly, "We've come this

far. Now I'm going to find that treasure, ghost or no ghost." He took a step forward. Instantly, someone chuckled and whispered again, "Beware. . . ."

Trixie frowned. "There's something about all this that isn't right at all. . . ."

The boys weren't listening. In another second, they had rushed past her toward the boulder's black shadows.

Trixie heard Mart shout, "Oh, wow, will you look at that! *What's going on?*"

Then there was silence.

Trixie wasn't sure what she expected to see when she raced forward to find them. She found herself thinking of the bats they had found in that other cave. It was strange, though, that this time the boys hadn't yelled a warning.

Moving carefully, she came to the place where the boys had disappeared. She rounded the corner and stopped dead.

The reality far surpassed anything she had imagined. She found the boys staring, speechless, at a small grotto in front of them. To add to their confusion, it seemed to be lit by invisible flickering torches. Trixie gazed around, looking for the source of the light, but she couldn't find it.

She saw long stalactites hanging from the

rocky roof, and from somewhere in the distance, she could hear the sound of ocean waves beating against some unseen shore.

Unbelieving, the boys were gazing at a small grass-covered island in the middle of the sandy floor. Even more astonishing was the tall palm tree that decorated its center.

"Gleeps!" Trixie exclaimed. "It's even got tropical flowers and plants growing at its base."

"Tropical flowers?" Honey breathed, running to join her. "In a cave?"

"I've never seen anything like it," Di cried a moment later.

"But that's not all," Dan said, pointing. "Will you look at that!"

Trixie gazed toward that surprising island and saw an old brass-studded wooden chest half hidden in the foliage. From its half-opened lid there sprawled a rope of gleaming pearls.

Propped against the chest was a grinning skeleton dressed in the clothes of a pirate chief.

In one bony hand he held a cutlass. In the other, he held a pistol. A dagger was stuck into the belt of his black trousers; the mace lay across his skinny lap.

"Oh, Trixie," Di gasped, "do you think it's Captain Trask?"

Then, as they stood rooted to the spot, the

skeleton opened its hideous mouth—and laughed.

Terrified, Honey and Di clung to each other and stared at the maker of the ghastly sound.

Even Mr. Appleton's dummy was affected by the skeleton's dreadful laughter. Momentarily unnerved, Mart relaxed his grip. For the second time that evening, Clarence dropped with a dull thud to the ground.

Honey and Di were beginning to feel that nothing had the power to astonish them anymore that night. They were wrong.

It seemed almost as though they were under the spell of some evil genius as they watched Clarence's head slowly detach itself from his un-protesting body. It seemed like fate when it rolled to the skeleton's feet.

But neither of them expected Trixie to walk casually forward to pick it up.

"I've been trying to tell you," she said, turning to face them. "It's a fake."

Di still hadn't recovered from the shock. "What's a fake?" she asked. "Are you talking about the dummy?"

"Of course not," Trixie answered impatiently. "I mean the cave, the ghostly voices, the sound of the sea—all of this." Holding Clarence's head in one hand, she gestured with it to indicate their surroundings.

"We guessed as much," Mart said slowly, "but all the same, you've got to admit the whole thing is wonderfully spooky."

"I don't know how it all works," Brian said, "but I'll bet there's some kind of electronic gimmick or something. I expect it's all turned on whenever anyone walks in here."

"How did you know, Trixie?" Honey asked.

"I got to thinking," Trixie answered, "and I guess the boys did, too. I realized that none of this whole situation rang true. When our flashlight went out, we shouldn't have been able to see a thing. Instead of that, the walls began to glow as if someone wanted to lead us here. Besides, it was all too easy. We didn't even have to search very far to find the cave."

"I wonder if they have that special lighting in here, too," Honey said suddenly. "If so, maybe the rocks as well as the galleon have been painted with fluorescent paint."

"The light could be coming from somewhere outside," Dan said uncertainly.

At that moment, Brian, who had been exploring, said, "No, I was right. The whole thing seems to be activated by a series of trip wires and switches. There even seems to be some sort of tape machine to give the sound effects. It's all hidden over here, behind this rock."

167

Mart stared down at the paper containing the clues to the treasure. "And I suppose there's one of these hidden somewhere in every room at the inn, too. Jeepers, it really had me going!"

"You know what this reminds me of?" Di said. "It's just like one of those big amusement parks where they feature attractions like the Tunnel of Love—"

"Or in this case, the Pirate's Cave," Mart broke in bitterly.

"But I still don't understand," Jim said. "Who's gone to the trouble of setting up such an elaborate joke?"

"Oh, I'm sure it's no joke," Trixie assured him. "I bet we'll find that this was all Mr. Trask's idea. I expect it's another one of his tourist attractions. He's fixed this up to give the place—"

"Atmosphere," Honey finished, grinning.

Trixie nodded. "And Di's right, I think. It *is* like one of those places where you have to pay admission to get in. Maybe, during the summer, they have tour guides and everything."

"But how about the treasure?" Di asked, still disappointed.

"Yeah, how about that?" Mart asked.

Trixie hesitated, then walked to the treasure chest and flipped open its lid. "Come and look," she invited, grinning.

The Bob-Whites crowded around.

"Well, I'll be a simian's sibling!" Mart exclaimed. "They look just like doubloons!"

Honey giggled as Trixie announced grandly, "It is chocolate! It is not very good chocolate, because I"—she thumped her chest with Clarence's head—"did not make it myself."

Clarence smiled patiently as Trixie and Honey told their friends how they, too, had made the same mistake earlier.

At last, they turned to leave. They paused for one final look around them. Now that they had solved the secret of the mysterious cave, they found themselves wondering how they had ever been fooled.

"Even the tree, the plants, and the skeleton were made of plastic," Mart said sadly as they made their way back to the beach.

"And don't forget the fake moss and squishy fungus on the walls," Trixie said, helping Mart rearrange Clarence across his shoulders.

It was fortunate that the fog had almost gone as the Bob-Whites made their way slowly back up the wooden steps.

When they reached the top of the cliff, Honey yawned. "I'm going straight to bed," she announced, "and this time nothing—not even the ghost of Captain Trask—is going to stop me."

Suddenly, Trixie felt very tired, too. So much had happened since they arrived at Pirate's Inn.

"Still, I'm glad we took the time to fit Clarence back together again," she told Honey later, as they climbed into bed. "I thought he looked terrific when we propped him up outside Mr. Appleton's door. He was almost as good as new."

"It still seems strange that a grown man should travel around with a manikin," Honey said sleepily as she snuggled under the covers. "Why does he, do you suppose?"

Trixie was thinking about something else. She stared up at the ceiling and said, "Tomorrow, Mr. Trask will tell us all about his disappearing trick. I can hardly wait to hear how he did it. Can you, Honey?"

But her friend was already fast asleep.

The Vanishing Trick • 16

IN THE MORNING, however, it took Trixie no time at all to learn that Mr. Trask was still missing.

"But what can have happened to him?" she asked as the Bob-Whites sat eating their breakfast.

Jim's fork, with its load of delicious blueberry pancake dripping with maple syrup, paused on its way to his mouth. "I wish I knew, Trix," he said. "There've been so many conflicting stories to account for his disappearance. The Weasel thinks he's made a quick unexpected trip to New York to order supplies of some sort. Smiley Jackson is certain that Mr. Trask's gone off somewhere to try to borrow money to pay off the loan—"

"The cash still hasn't turned up," Dan interrupted, "and it's supposed to be paid to Mr. Morgan tonight."

Trixie stared out of the dining room window. Although the last faint traces of fog still remained, she could tell that the sun was about to break through.

Di passed her the tray containing the mouthwatering assortment of pancake syrups. They were neatly labeled *maple*, *raspberry*, *strawberry*, *blueberry*, and *honey*. Trixie gazed at the sparkling glass containers without seeing them. She was thinking hard.

"What about Miss Trask?" she asked at last. "What does she think has happened to her brother?"

Mart sighed and pushed his empty plate away from him. "I think she's called the police," he said. "She thinks there may be dirty work at the crossroads."

Trixie looked up quickly. "What kind of dirty work?"

"That's just it, Trix," Honey replied. "She's not sure. In fact, no one's sure about anything except that a lot of money that should be here isn't, and that—"

"And that Mr. Trask shouldn't have disappeared, but he did," Brian added.

"While the rest of you sack artists were still snoring," Jim announced, grinning, "we men got up early and really made a thorough search for the missing cash." He frowned. "I wish I knew what we ought to do next."

"We told Miss Trask about the cave and the ship," Dan put in. "We even took her down to the beach to take a look around."

"Why didn't you wait for us?" Trixie asked.

Jim smiled at her. "You didn't miss anything, Trix. As you know, we couldn't go on board the galleon. We didn't even walk along the jetty. Remember those signs? They told us to keep off, in no uncertain terms."

Trixie stared up at the villainous-looking portrait of the fake Captain Trask. He seemed to leer back at her.

"I hate that picture," she said suddenly. "I wish we could see what the real captain looked like. Do you think Miss Trask would let us see the original painting?"

After breakfast, when they went to ask her, they discovered her sitting in the little office that belonged to her brother, staring out at the pale sunshine.

Although she greeted them with her usual kind

173

patience, the Bob-Whites could tell she was very worried.

"Oh, Miss Trask," Honey said, hurrying to her side, "is there any news?"

Miss Trask sighed. "I've just had a visit from the police," she said. "They seem to think there's nothing to worry about. They've promised to make inquiries. They're interviewing the staff now."

"Is there anything we can do?" Jim asked, his voice low.

Miss Trask smiled at the circle of concerned young faces around her. "There certainly is," she said briskly. "You can go and enjoy yourselves until it's time to eat again. As I expect you've guessed, Gaston is back in his kitchen, so that's one thing less to trouble us."

"We came to ask you if we could see the real portrait of Captain Trask," Trixie said.

"You could if I knew where it was," Miss Trask answered promptly. "It's funny that you should ask. I've looked for it myself, but I can't find it anywhere."

"Things do seem to have a peculiar habit of disappearing around here," Trixie said without thinking.

"What a dumb thing to say!" Mart exclaimed when they had left the room.

"It really was," Brian agreed. "Miss Trask was already upset. You might not help thinking such a thing, but you didn't have to *say* it."

Trixie knew that Mart and Brian were still angry with her as the Bob-Whites discussed what they were going to do for the rest of the morning. They ignored her suggestion that they should try searching again for either Mr. Trask or the missing money.

"Now that the police are on the job," Brian said, "they won't want a bunch of amateurs like us getting in their way."

In the end, the Bob-Whites spent the balance of that Saturday morning exploring the little town of Pirate's Point. They wandered along the main street, with its rows of quaint little stores and small houses with pocket-handkerchief-sized front yards.

If Trixie had not been worried about what they would find when they returned to the inn, she might have enjoyed the visit. As it was, she couldn't shake off her conviction that something more was about to happen—and soon.

One anxious glance at Miss Trask's face, when at last they returned, did nothing to reassure her.

"No," Miss Trask said, trying to smile as she met them at the front door, "there's no news of my brother. The police are still making inquiries, but—" she bit her lip—"they seem to feel that he's disappeared as some sort of publicity stunt."

Trixie stared. "But why would he do that?"

"I'm afraid it was something one of the waiters said that gave them the idea," Miss Trask answered. "I believe it's quite true that Frank has thought up a lot of ideas recently to promote Pirate's Inn."

"I'll bet it was Weasel Willis who told the police it was just a publicity stunt," Trixie told Honey and Di later, as they trudged upstairs after lunch.

"But maybe he's right, Trix," Di said.

Trixie hoped with all her heart that he was. "All the same," she said, "I can't help thinking that if we could only solve that other disappearance—the one where Captain Trask vanished—it might help us figure out what happened last night. When the lunch rush is over, let's search the dining room again."

Honey groaned. "Oh, no! I don't think I could stand it."

"Me, either," Di announced. "And there isn't anything you can say that will make me change my mind, Trixie."

Thirty minutes later, the three girls were on their hands and knees under the captain's table, searching for a secret trapdoor.

Suddenly a familiar voice drawled, "My, my! And what have we here? I *was* going to say that great minds think alike, except I know one of them is a pea-brain."

Trixie stuck out her head and glared up at Mart. Brian, Jim, and Dan stood behind him.

"Pea-brain yourself!" Trixie snapped, her cheeks red. "And what are you doing here? Don't tell me; I can guess. You're here to find out about the disappearing trick. Don't bother to deny it."

"But I don't have to find out about it," Mart drawled in an infuriatingly smug voice. "You see, I know how it was done."

Honey gasped and scrambled to her feet. "You do? You really do?"

"Of course he doesn't." Trixie was scornful. "He's just showing off."

"Now, Trix," Di said, crawling out from under the table, "you don't mean that."

Mart flushed. "Yes, she does. And just for that, I won't say another word. Go ahead and figure it out for yourself, *little* sister. I tell you I know how Captain Trask must have vanished. You would, too, if you stopped to think about it." He flung himself into the nearest chair, crossed his arms, and closed his mouth tightly.

"For crying out loud, you two," Brian said,

sighing deeply, "why can't you get along?"

"Mart was just about to show us how it was done," Dan told Trixie.

"Oh, who needs him," Trixie said, turning away impatiently. "If he can figure it out, we can, too. All we have to do is find the secret trapdoor—"

"Wrong," Mart sang out.

"Or a hidden passage," Trixie went on, ignoring him.

"Wrong again," Mart said, forgetting his vow of silence. "You're not even close. For your information, Lucy Snodgrass, I've been asking around, and guess what I found out? This ancient domicile has been plagued periodically by the soft-bodied insect of the order Isoptera."

Trixie stared. "The *what?*"

"They've had termites," Brian explained.

"But what has that got to do with anything?" Trixie cried. "Are you trying to tell us that Captain Trask was carried away by *termites?*"

Jim laughed. "I think Mart's trying to tell us that because the floorboards were riddled with termites, they must have been replaced many times since the inn was first built. Maybe parts of the paneling were, too. Am I right?"

Trixie let out her breath in one long sigh. Of course he was right! Why hadn't she thought of that? The Weasel had practically told her the same thing only yesterday, except that she hadn't been paying attention.

"If the floorboards have been replaced," Honey said, "and if the paneling has, too, then how come they've never found a secret passage?"

"Because there never was one to find," Mart answered at once. "The captain didn't disappear that way at all."

"Then how did he do it?" Trixie asked.

At this point, Mart, suddenly remembering that he wasn't talking to her, infuriatingly refused to say another word.

"It's really quite simple," a quiet voice said behind them. Trixie turned and saw sandy-haired Mr. Appleton smiling at them. "I came to find you to thank you all for rescuing Clarence last night," he said. "Also, I thought I might find you here. The legend of the vanishing pirate really is a brainteaser, don't you think?"

"But you know the answer?" Trixie asked.

Mr. Appleton chuckled. "Let's say I *think* I know the answer. I suppose no one will ever really be sure about it."

"I am," Mart muttered. "It's the oldest magic trick in the book. I should have recognized it as soon as I heard the story."

"The way the legend goes," Mr. Appleton said,

179

"is that the soldiers arrived and surrounded the table. But suppose Captain Trask already knew of his impending arrest. And suppose he made arrangements of his own."

"Like what?" Dan asked.

"Like bribing the soldiers ahead of time," Mr. Appleton answered promptly. "If it had been me, I'd have already arranged to have a soldier's uniform handy. Or maybe had one of the soldiers bring one with him. Then, when I was about to be arrested, I'd have merely slipped it on over what I was wearing—"

"And the captain was in his shirt sleeves at the time," Honey gasped.

"I get it," Trixie breathed. "Then the captain merely joined the soldiers as they backed away from the table, and he just walked out of the inn with them. And that must be what Mr. Trask meant when he said he discovered the answer when he was looking at his own costume."

She was still thinking about it when Mr. Appleton had gone.

"Is that the way you figured it out, Mart?" Di asked.

"It sure was," Mart said. "It was the only way it could have happened."

"But I was hoping it would help us figure out how Mr. Trask disappeared," Trixie cried.

"It's too bad it doesn't," Jim said later, as they stood outside the dining room. "But one thing's certain, Trix. Mr. Appleton's so clever at solving puzzles, you should have gotten him to help you with the other one."

Trixie frowned. "What other one?"

Jim grinned. "What color was the bear?"

Trixie grinned back at him. "What three words are most used by morons?" she asked.

Jim stared. "I don't know."

"You're right, Jim," Trixie answered, giggling. "And I don't know about the bear, either. But I will."

All the same, she crossed her fingers. She knew she was going to need all the luck she could get—and not just with the bear.

More Worries · 17

AS THE DAY WORE ON, Trixie found herself growing more and more uneasy. Everyone guessed that Miss Trask was, too, though she did her best to hide it.

She had listened quietly to the Bob-Whites' excited account of what must have happened to the wily old captain so many years before. She had congratulated them warmly on having solved the ancient mystery. Then she had urged them all to go and enjoy themselves.

"After all," she said, "there's nothing more we can do now except wait."

Trixie had gone reluctantly with her friends to

explore the surrounding countryside. Even an enchanting drive through parts of the beautiful Catskill Mountains had failed to arouse her interest, however.

It was dusk when the Bob-Whites returned to the inn. Trixie was glad to scramble out of the station wagon and run indoors, but in no time at all, she was back.

"There's still no word from Mr. Trask," she told her friends breathlessly. "Even the police seem to have given up. They still expect him to return in time to grab the headlines in tomorrow's newspapers."

"Yeah," Dan said, climbing out of the car, "I can see it all now: HISTORY REPEATS ITSELF. SECOND MAN VANISHES FROM MYSTERIOUS INN."

"There's something we haven't really thought of," Trixie said slowly. "Just suppose Mr. Trask didn't mean to vanish."

Honey rolled down her window and stared up at her friend. "You mean, you think he's been kidnapped?"

Trixie nodded. "Can you think of a better explanation for what's happened?"

Mart clambered out of his seat and glared down at his sister. "Oh, for crying out loud, Trix! That's the craziest thing I ever heard."

Jim, at the wheel, frowned. "No, wait," he

said. "Let's hear what Trixie has to say."

"The whole thing just sounds so strange to me," Trixie began. "We know that Mr. Trask was really looking forward to this weekend. He invited his sister here specially, didn't he? We also know he'd borrowed a lot of money from wealthy Mr. Morgan, and he was about to pay it back."

"But we don't know that for sure," Honey pointed out. "Some people think he doesn't have the money to pay back."

"But if he didn't have it," Trixie said carefully, "why did he invite his sister here to celebrate? I thought the whole idea was to show her what a success he's made of the inn. We've seen for ourselves how popular it is."

"And now that he's set up the cave and the ship," Di murmured thoughtfully, "it'll be more of a tourist attraction than ever."

"It's so popular," Jim said, "that one of the big hotel chains has been after Mr. Trask to sell out to them. They're willing to pay plenty."

"I didn't know that, Jim!" Trixie cried.

"Gaston told me," Jim explained.

"If that's true," Brian said, "then it might be to someone's advantage to try to make Mr. Trask sell Pirate's Inn."

"Suppose," Trixie answered, "that the hotel

chain sent someone here. And suppose that someone tried to make trouble by—"

"By causing odd accidents during the summer," Honey put in excitedly, "and setting a fire in a guest's bedroom—"

"See?" Trixie said. "The idea's not so crazy!"

Dan was still frowning. "Even if all that's true, it still doesn't help us know what happened to Mr. Trask."

"But what if the spy, or whoever it is who's working for the hotel chain, managed to steal all of Mr. Trask's money from Pirate's Inn?" Trixie asked. "He tried to rob the place before, remember? And what if Mr. Trask had just found out who the thief was? He was about to tell us, when Mr. X—"

"Who's Mr. X?" Mart interrupted.

"I'm coming to that," Trixie said impatiently. "Mr. Trask was about to unmask the villain when he was kidnapped."

"Here we go again," Mart exclaimed. "It's another Lucy Snodgrass plot. Anyway, Mr. Trask wasn't about to unmask anybody. He was going to explain how Captain Trask disappeared. Then he was going to show us the galleon. I suppose you've already decided whom to accuse as Mr. X."

"Weasel Willis," Trixie announced. "I'm certain of it. The hotel chain has paid him to cause trouble. And that's just what he's done. I think we ought to call the police."

"And tell them what?" Mart asked.

"Tell them what we suspect, of course," Trixie answered.

Brian was shaking his head. "It's a nice theory, Trixie, but you can't *prove* any of it. You don't *know* that there really is any money missing. You don't *know* that the hotel chain has been causing trouble. And you have no reason to suspect Weasel Willis of anything."

"Jeepers!" Trixie exclaimed. "What more do you want?"

"Proof, Trix," Dan said, joining Brian and Mart in the driveway.

Brian sighed and turned away. "I'm going to wash up for dinner," he said. "How about you guys?"

While Jim parked the station wagon, Mart pulled a crumpled tissue from his pocket. Gravely he presented it to his frowning sister. "Don't cry because we don't like your theories, Trix," he said solemnly. "Take this instead. It may not be good for the sniffles, but it will sure help soften the *blow*."

Trixie could hear him still laughing at his own joke as he and the other boys disappeared behind the doors to Pirate's Inn.

186

"Oh, that Mart!" Trixie told Di. "Sometimes he makes me so mad!"

"Are you going to keep an eye on the Weasel?" Honey asked.

"I sure am," Trixie said stubbornly. Then, when the three girls were in the lobby, she added, "I'm going to stick so close to him that he'll think he's grown an extra shadow."

Just then the door to the office opened and upset all her plans.

Trixie stood as if frozen to the spot as she heard a man's deep voice say, "Believe me, Marge, I'd do anything to help you and Frank. You know that. Why, we've known each other for too long for me to do anything else."

Trixie could tell it was Mr. Morgan, who held the mortgage on the inn.

"Don't be like that, Marge," she heard him say. "I'd give you more time if I could, but it just isn't possible. And it was Frank himself who set the deadline. Tonight at seven, he said, and that's what was agreed on."

"If only it weren't such a very large amount of money," Miss Trask said, "I might have been able to raise it from somewhere." She paused, then continued briskly, "But that isn't your problem. It's mine now. I know that. It's just that Pirate's Inn has been in our family for so long—"

"Ah, Marge," Mr. Morgan said from the door, "if only I were as rich as everyone thinks I am. As it is, I've had several investments go sour on me recently, and I really need the cash myself. Listen, you've still got an hour to come up with something."

"I'm afraid it's too late," Miss Trask replied, her voice tight. "If you'll come back at seven, I'll be prepared then to hand over the deed."

In another moment, the office door had closed firmly behind him, and Mr. Morgan stood staring at the three girls who were standing there.

"It's sad," he muttered to himself as he hurried through the front door. "It's really sad."

"Oh, Trix," Honey cried, truly realizing for the first time that Miss Trask was about to lose her childhood home, "isn't there anything that we can do?"

"Yes," Di added eagerly, "maybe I could phone my father—"

Honey was shaking her head. "Even if your dad or mine was willing to lend the money, Miss Trask is too proud to take it. Besides, we could never get the cash here in time. The deadline's in an hour."

"I'll think of something," Di announced. "What's more, I'll go and talk to the boys. Maybe they'll have some ideas of their own."

188

Honey watched her hurry upstairs, then she turned to say something to Trixie.

The words died on her lips. Her friend's face wore such a strange expression. She looked dazed, almost as though she had been hit over the head.

"What is it?" Honey cried. "Oh, Trixie! Did you remember something?"

"It's the craziest thing," Trixie answered at last, "and I don't know why I didn't think of it before. Oh, Honey, you're never going to believe it! But I've just realized where we're going to find Mr. Trask!"

Disaster! • 18

TRIXIE DIDN'T STOP to explain. In the next instant, she was moving so fast that Honey had a hard time keeping up with her.

Outside the inn, Trixie stopped abruptly. The pale moon was just beginning to turn everything to silver.

For a moment, Honey thought her friend was going to chase after Mr. Morgan, who was just driving away. But Trixie had quite a different plan in mind.

Puzzled, Honey saw her flip the light switches by the front door and then race across the grass toward the edge of the cliff.

By the time Honey had reached her side, Trixie was staring down at the river. Even though Honey knew that the galleon was not a ghostly one after all, the sight of it still made her shiver. It glowed and shimmered in the water as if it were waiting to take phantom passengers to another world.

All at once, Honey frowned as she fixed her gaze on the proud figurehead on the ship's bow. She could hardly believe her eyes. There was no question about it. The lady *was* crying. Mournful tears were rolling down her cheeks.

"Why," she gasped, bewildered, "you were right all along, Trix. But what does it mean?"

Trixie was gazing at the lady, too. "It means," she replied slowly, "that I've just realized those tears are really fluorescent paint, Honey. That's why we can't see them in ordinary light."

"I still don't understand," Honey said. "What are you looking for now?"

Trixie was searching the grass close to the wooden steps that led down to the beach. "I'm looking for signs of a ghostly visitor," she said at last.

"What?" Honey's eyes were wide.

"I mean the footprints we saw last night," Trixie explained. "They should be here somewhere, too." She pounced. "They are! Look,

191

Honey, they're faint, but we can still see them."

Her friend stared. "Are you trying to tell me that these are just fluorescent paint, too?"

Trixie nodded. "I'm sure of it. I'm also sure of something else. Someone's been on that boat— and recently! Honey, we're going down there to take a look."

Before Honey could say another word, Trixie was already moving toward the steps and hurrying down them. Honey groaned as she quickly followed.

Soon the two girls were once more standing on the tiny beach.

"Listen, Honey," Trixie said. "Last night *before* dinner, we saw the ship, right?"

Honey nodded.

"Do you remember the figurehead?" Trixie asked. "I saw it, and the lady wasn't crying. Then later, after Mr. Trask disappeared, Gaston showed us the ship, and suddenly the lady had paint running down her face. *Where did it come from?*"

"Maybe one of the workmen—" Honey began uncertainly.

"But there weren't any workmen here," Trixie said, moving gingerly toward the jetty. "Come on, Honey. There's something funny about all this, and it's up to us to find out what it is."

Honey saw the signs that said: DANGER! KEEP OUT! AUTHORIZED PERSONNEL ONLY.

She hoped the words would make Trixie pause, but her friend rushed right past them as if they didn't exist. Her gaze was fixed on the huge, shining bulk of the galleon, and soon it loomed above them.

They could hear tiny waves lapping quietly around it. They could see every detail of its wooden hull. A gangway led to its upper deck, and in no time at all, Trixie was running toward it. After a moment's hesitation, Honey followed.

Once on board, the two girls stood looking around them. They could see the repairs that were being made. Part of the deck was obviously being replaced. Long timbers were stretched across gaping holes, and cans of paint stood waiting, like rows of tin soldiers.

Above their heads, the tall masts creaked and swayed in the evening breeze. The sails were neatly furled against the yardarms.

"Jeepers!" Trixie breathed. "How wonderful it is. I almost wish I were a pirate. Imagine setting sail in a galleon like this."

For a moment, Trixie and Honey forgot why they were there. They picked their way carefully across the deck. Then they stared, enchanted, at the twinkling lights on the opposite shore. They imagined that they were just arriving at some exotic foreign land.

Lost in daydreams, neither of them noticed the figure, dressed in a pirate's costume, watching from the cliffs behind them. They didn't see him suddenly hurry down the wooden steps. Undetected, he raced along the jetty.

Then, just as he reached the top of the gangway, some small noise made Trixie swing around.

She gasped. He was rushing toward them across the deck, his hands outstretched. "You nosy kids!" he snarled. "So you found out we kidnapped Frank Trask, huh? Well, we got rid of him! Now I'll get rid of you, too! You should've stayed home where you belong!"

Almost without thinking, Trixie pushed Honey away from her, to safety. She stood facing the pirate alone.

As she gazed at him, her heart thumping, she wondered how he had ever fooled her for a moment. His lips were twisted in a triumphant sneer as he reached for her.

Honey stood horrified. In another second, his hands would close around Trixie's throat.

Then, instinctively, Trixie ducked away. After that, everything happened at once.

The pirate was moving so fast that he couldn't

stop. He stumbled over a long, loose, wooden plank that stuck way out over the side of the ship. He tottered for a few steps and tried to regain his balance. He failed.

With his arms and legs vainly flailing the air, he walked the plank! Then he dropped straight over the side. He hit the water with a mighty splash, and the Hudson River closed over his head.

As he surfaced a moment later and swam away with powerful strokes, Honey let out her breath in a long, shaky sigh.

"Why," she said, staring after him until he was out of sight, "I simply don't believe it! The villain all along was Smiley Jackson!"

"Don't feel bad about it," Trixie said as they moved unsteadily away from the side of the ship. "He fooled me, too. I thought he was such a nice man."

"So he was the spy, after all," Honey exclaimed.

"He sure was," Trixie answered. "I'm sure he's been the cause of all the inn's troubles these last few months. Twice he tried to steal Mr. Trask's money, and I'll bet we'll find he was the one who unlocked Mr. Appleton's door with a master key and set the fire yesterday."

"But what did he mean when he told us he'd got rid of Mr. Trask?" Honey asked.

"I think he meant just that," Trixie said. "I told you I suspected something. Mr. Trask didn't mean to disappear. Smiley Jackson kidnapped him. He took advantage of all the confusion when Weasel Willis dropped the cake."

"I remember now," Honey said slowly. "Smiley was missing from the dining room for a long time last night. Do you think he had it all planned?"

"I don't know," Trixie confessed. "Maybe Weasel dropped the cake on purpose. Or maybe Smiley did it all on the spur of the moment. Anyway, I think Mr. Trask is right here on this ship. It's the only place that makes any sense."

Honey watched as her friend gazed uncertainly toward the bow.

"Mr. Trask?" Trixie shouted. "Can you hear me? Where are you?"

A low moan answered her.

In another instant, the two girls were racing toward a shapeless bundle that lay under a tarpaulin in the ship's bow.

"I should have known it long before this," Trixie said as she gently pulled the cover away.

There, right above the figurehead of the ship, lay a bearded man, bound and gagged. Frank Trask had been found!

While Trixie untied him, Honey picked up a

can of fluorescent paint that had lain on its side next to him.

"I managed to kick the paint can over," he explained later, breathing hard. "It happened just as they were tying me up. I hoped it would attract someone's attention."

"It sure did," Honey answered. "Trixie noticed it at once. The spilled paint ran down the figurehead's face, you see. It made us think the lady was crying."

"I am awfully glad you were curious about it," Mr. Trask told Trixie as he rubbed his wrists. "I still don't know who kidnapped me or why they brought me here. But I *do* know that I'm mighty obliged to you."

Trixie's face was red with embarrassment. She never liked to be thanked for the things she felt were simply right to do. She was just extremely thankful that he had been found.

"Why do you say 'they' brought you here?" Honey asked. "How many of them were there?"

"There were two," Frank Trask answered promptly. "And once I get my hands on the pair, I'm going to make 'em into yesterday's hash! They jumped me as I walked into the kitchen after all that commotion with the dropped cake. I was going to lend a hand, y'see, to help clear it up. But someone dropped a tablecloth over my

197

head—and the next thing I knew, here I was!"

"I still don't think any of this was planned," Trixie said, thinking hard. "If it had been, they'd have rushed you away to some other hiding place." She went on to explain to Mr. Trask all that had happened since the previous evening.

Mr. Trask was astonished when he discovered that one of his assailants was none other than his trusted waiter, Smiley Jackson.

"I think I know who the other man is," Trixie murmured, "but it would help a lot if you could identify him."

Mr. Trask was unable to help her. He said he hadn't seen anyone at all.

Honey couldn't help smiling. "I expect the kidnappers were hoping to transfer their prisoner somewhere else," she remarked. "But what with all the excitement around here last night, we didn't give them the chance."

Soon Mr. Trask felt well enough to move. "So some people think I don't have the money to pay back my loan, eh?" he said at last. "But let me tell you, me hearties—I do! And it's in a safe place."

Trixie helped him to his feet. "I don't want to hurry you," she said, "but it's almost seven o'clock. Mr. Morgan will be waiting for you."

Honey, remembering, gasped. "Jeepers! And if

we don't get there pretty fast, Miss Trask will hand over the deed to Pirate's Inn."

"What's that you say?" Mr. Trask roared. "No one's going to hand over anything! Quickly, ladies, we've got to get to the inn at once!"

Impetuously, he raced toward the head of the gangway.

"Oh, Mr. Trask, be careful!" Trixie cried.

It was too late!

In the next moment, as the girls watched, unbelieving, disaster struck. He tripped over a workman's toolbox left carelessly in the middle of the deck. As Smiley Jackson had done minutes before, he tried and failed to regain his balance.

Then, before the girls could take even one step to help him, he fell heavily to the deck and lay quite still.

A Villain Unmasked • 19

GLEEPS!" Trixie cried. "He knocked himself out!"

Honey dropped to her knees beside the unconscious man. "Oh, Trixie," she whimpered, "what are we going to do? I thought we'd won. In another few minutes, we'd have been at the inn. But now the Trasks are going to lose everything they own!"

"Wait!" Trixie said excitedly. "I've just had an idea. Honey, will you stay here while I run for help?"

"Of course I will," her friend answered at once. "But it's too late to save Pirate's Inn. Even Brian can't revive Mr. Trask in time. And we don't know where he's hidden the money, anyway. Oh, why did this have to happen now?"

Trixie was already picking her way across the deck. In no time at all, she was racing along the jetty. When she had almost reached the inn, she looked up at the windows on the second floor. In another instant, she was sounding the Bob-Whites' secret call for help. *Bob, bob-white. Bob, bob-white.*

A window flew open immediately. Trixie could almost have fainted with relief when she saw Mart's blond head gazing down at her. In an emergency, Trixie knew there was no one else she would rather have by her side—unless it was Jim.

My almost-twin and I are alike in so many ways, she told herself. *Maybe that's why we're always arguing.* She made up her mind right then to be more patient when he teased her.

She wondered if this weekend had also taught Miss Trask a lesson. Trixie suspected that she, too, had discovered that a brother was often a pretty nice person to have around.

Breathlessly, Trixie explained to Mart all that had happened. He didn't need to be told twice how serious the situation was.

Moments later, the rest of the Bob-Whites had gathered to listen to Trixie's plan. Then, as they were talking, they saw Mr. Morgan's shiny black

201

limousine driving toward Pirate's Inn. There wasn't a second to lose!

Brian and Dan raced toward the galleon to help Honey with the injured man.

"We'll be back to help you as soon as we can," Brian yelled over his shoulder.

Di, too, didn't hesitate. She rushed indoors to call for an ambulance and for the police. Mart was right on her heels.

Jim and Trixie also hurried inside. There was only one more thing left to do. Trixie knew that if she had guessed wrong, her mistake would affect the Trasks for the rest of their lives.

Jim knew it, too. "Are you sure this is going to work, Trix?" he asked her.

"It's got to," Trixie answered grimly. "Oh, Jim, it's simply got to!"

The inn's old-fashioned clock showed exactly one minute to seven when Mr. Nicholas Morgan walked into the dining room.

What he saw there made him stop dead. The captain's table was set for dinner, as it had been the evening before. Seated around it was a group of people, staring at him. He could see Trixie, Jim, Di, and Mart. Miss Trask, tight-lipped, was sitting beside a man dressed in a very familiar costume.

Although the man's back was to the door, Nicholas Morgan could tell that his clothes were those of a pirate chief. In front of him on the table lay neat stacks of money.

Frank Trask was about to pay off his loan, after all!

The pirate chief didn't turn around. "Come in, Nick," he said gruffly. "We've been waiting for you. It's too bad your plan didn't work. I managed to get here in time, as you can see."

Mr. Morgan took a step toward him. *"Frank?"* he said incredulously. "B-But that's impossible! You're supposed to be—"

"Kidnapped?" Miss Trask asked icily. "Is that what you were about to say, Nick?"

Nicholas Morgan tried to gather his scattered wits. "I don't know what you're talking about," he muttered.

"Oh, I think you do," Miss Trask snapped. "My brother just told me all about it. Smiley Jackson caused a great deal of trouble here at Pirate's Inn, but he was just following your orders, wasn't he? *You* are the one who wanted Frank to lose this place so that you could sell it to the hotel chain. You really did need the money, didn't you? Well, your plan failed!"

Mr. Morgan looked at the circle of grave faces watching him. "What is this?" he sneered. "I've never heard such a lot of nonsense! If Frank told you I kidnapped him, he's simply telling you another one of his stories. Why, even the police think he disappeared as a publicity stunt!"

"It won't work, Nick," the pirate chief answered. "Last night you came to the inn early to see if Smiley Jackson had been successful in his second robbery attempt. When I walked into the kitchen unexpectedly, you took advantage of a golden opportunity, kidnapping me and holding me prisoner on board the galleon."

"But I wasn't anywhere near the galleon last night," Mr. Morgan blustered. "In fact, I've never been anywhere near it."

"That's not true," Trixie said quietly. "You see, I saw your shoes. You had fluorescent paint all over them. When Honey and I met you near the picnic tables, your shoes glowed when Mart turned on the lights. You made footprints in the grass, too. I remembered tonight that the only place you could have picked up the paint was on the ship, where Mr. Trask spilled it."

There was silence. Then Nicholas Morgan snarled, "You'll never prove this in a court of law. I'll destroy those shoes before anyone else can see them. And when I've done that, I'll sue you all for slander. I'll—"

He reached to the table to grab the money.

But in the next instant, he stood horrified. The sleeve of his coat had brushed against the pirate chief's shoulder—and Frank Trask's head fell off!

Completely unnerved, Nicholas Morgan spun around and started to run toward the door.

"Stop him!" Trixie cried. "Don't let him get away!"

Immediately, Mart and Jim rose to their feet and rushed toward him, but they didn't see Weasel Willis, who had been making his way slowly toward them. In his hands he was carrying Gaston's latest creation—another beautiful three-tiered cake.

Then Mart stumbled and lurched sideways. He clutched at Jim. Jim clutched at Weasel. And no one ever quite believed what happened next.

Weasel's feet shot out from under him. The cake soared high into the air. While everyone watched, speechless with astonishment, it landed on Nicholas Morgan's head.

Half-blinded by the sticky mess, he tried to grope his way toward the dining room exit—and walked straight into the arms of the police.

Gravely, Trixie picked something up from the floor. It was this that had so fortunately tripped Mart. Sticking it back on the pirate chief's shoulders, where it belonged, she grinned.

"I'm glad it was only Clarence who lost his

head," she told her delighted audience.

Then she joined in the happy laughter that followed.

"I don't know how you ever thought of using the dummy to trick Morgan into a confession," Mr. Trask said, two hours later.

He sat in his place at the captain's table, surrounded by his friends. Marvin Appleton had also joined them. After all, it had been his dummy who had helped capture the villain!

Apart from a slight bump on the head, the doctor had pronounced Mr. Trask none the worse for his adventure.

"Trixie solved the whole mystery herself this time," Mart announced. "For once our schoolgirl shamus was really clicking along on all four cylinders."

Trixie's face was red. "It wasn't anything," she mumbled, "and it wouldn't have worked if Mart hadn't made Clarence talk."

"But it *was* something," Di insisted. "If you hadn't guessed where Mr. Trask had hidden the money, the inn would belong to that awful Mr. Morgan right now."

"That's right," Mr. Trask boomed. "How did you know where to find it, Trixie?"

"I got to remembering that old riddle," Trixie

replied, "where a rooster lays an egg exactly in the middle of a gabled roof. One side of the roof is painted red, the other blue. So—on which side of the roof did the egg fall?"

Honey frowned. "What do gabled roofs have to do with where you found the money?"

"The answer to both problems is very simple once you've figured it out—" Trixie began.

Before she could finish, Weasel Willis was by her side. "Gaston wants you to have this as a reward," he announced, presenting her with the largest hot fudge sundae she had ever seen.

There was something different about the Weasel, but Trixie couldn't figure out what it was. This new puzzle distracted her attention from Honey's question.

Mr. Trask chuckled and said, "You'll be glad to know that Weasel's put away his eye patch forever. He really does have two good eyes. He was just using the patch and his stubbly chin for—"

"Atmosphere!" everyone shouted.

Trixie felt sorry that she had ever suspected the Weasel of wrongdoing. She knew she would have to learn not to judge by appearances alone.

On the other hand, everything had turned out wonderfully for Miss Trask. She and Trixie had recently had a private talk. Trixie knew now that

207

she had been dreading her visit to Pirate's Point. She had quarreled with her brother many months ago, but now they had made up and were friends once more. And now that Pirate's Inn was paid for, Mr. Trask could even help with their invalid sister's hospital bills.

"And the police have caught Smiley Jackson," Miss Trask announced. "He's confessed everything, even to setting the fire. He wouldn't have let the inn burn, of course. He was just trying to cause the last in a series of 'accidents' to force Frank to give up."

"I still don't understand how Mr. Morgan and Smiley hoped to get away with kidnapping you," Di told Mr. Trask.

"I'm sure," Trixie said, "that they would have denied everything. And they would have let their prisoner go, once they owned the inn, and Mr. Trask couldn't have proved anything."

Honey turned to Mr. Appleton and asked, "What *do* you use Clarence for?"

Mr. Appleton looked uncomfortable. "I really do use him in my work," he said. "You see, I'm a writer, and Clarence helps me figure out some of my action scenes. Last night, for instance, when you saw us on top of the cliff, Lucy was supposed to be struggling for her life with a foreign spy—"

Trixie gasped. *"Lucy!* Are you *Lucy Radcliffe?"*

As Mr. Appleton nodded, Mart shouted with laughter. "Eighteen years old and has a peaches-and-cream complexion!" he yelled.

But it was Trixie's turn to laugh when Mr. Appleton added, "I'm also Cosmo McNaught. I write science-fiction stuff, too. Perhaps you've heard of me."

Brian chuckled. "Oh, they've both heard of you, all right. You're sitting next to two of your greatest fans."

Trixie was still trying to recover from the shock when Honey said, "We found a scary note that said Trixie was being watched."

Marvin Appleton chuckled. "It was mine. I was doodling around with another story idea just before the fire, and I must have accidentally dropped it when I changed rooms. Incidentally, I was glad that you rescued my latest manuscript. It was in the desk drawer."

Jim sighed. "Now all Trixie has to do is to solve the final mystery."

Mr. Appleton looked puzzled. "What mystery is that?"

"You're standing in a house," Honey began.

"The house has windows on all four sides," Dan added.

"Every window faces south," Di chimed in.

"A quadrupedal animal of the family Ursidae

walks by," Mart said. "Now, the question is, What color is the bear?"

Trixie laughed. "I figured that out, too! The bear was white. The only place in the world where all windows can face south is the North Pole."

"Of course!" Honey exclaimed. "I should have known."

"And I," Trixie said, finally returning to the subject of the missing money, "should have known that enormous paintings can't disappear into thin air. I finally figured out that the original portrait of the real Captain Trask must be behind the fake one. And that's where I found the missing money—in between the two thicknesses of canvas. We'd looked everywhere else."

"After that attempted robbery," Mr. Trask murmured, "I couldn't think of a better place to keep it. And I did tell you he was guarding the family treasure."

Jim frowned. "I still don't know on which side of the roof the egg fell."

"The red side," Mart said promptly.

"The blue one," Brian sang out, grinning.

Trixie smiled affectionately at them both. "You've forgotten that some questions have very easy answers," she teased.

"In the same way that wooden figureheads

can't really cry?" Honey asked mischievously.

"And wily old pirates can't really vanish?" Miss Trask added, smiling at her brother.

"And as far as I know," Trixie said, giggling, "roosters never lay eggs."

Everyone laughed as Mr. Appleton raised his glass of punch. "You know, Trixie," he said, "I envy you. You lead such an exciting life."

The Bob-Whites smiled at Trixie's flushed face. It was thanks to her, they knew, that they all led exciting lives.

"In fact," Honey whispered, "I can hardly wait for our next mysterious adventure."

"And neither," said Trixie happily, "can I!"